Dead Ringer

"Jesus," the man whispered, "it's like seeing a ghost!"

He was staring at me. He was a huge black man who was shoehorned into a pale gray suit. Most of his face was beard.

"Her eyes, Jeannie! It's Silk all over again." He seemed so emotional, but my mother's face was stone cold. So this was about my father. I felt a little rush of excitement.

"Do I look that much like him?" I asked.

"Dead ringer," he said. And he was gone.

I followed Mom through the living room into our bedroom. She went directly to the mirror and concentrated on fixing the wisps of blond hair that had escaped.

"What was that all about?" I asked.

"Your father's dead," she said.

Other Borzoi Sprinters you will enjoy

Looking On by Betty Miles
Matt's Crusade by Margot Marek
The Ruby in the Smoke by Philip Pullman
Shadow in the North by Philip Pullman
The Watch House by Robert Westall

Blues FOR SILK GARCIA

Erika Tamar

BORZOI SPRINTERS • ALFRED A. KNOPF
NEW YORK

for Monica, Ray and Michael

Library of Congress Catalog Card Number: 82-25259
ISBN: 0-679-80424-2
RL: 5.1
First Borzoi Sprinter edition: February 1991

Manufactured in the United States of America
10 9 8 7 6 5 4 3 2 1

Prologue

I am center stage now. I cannot see beyond the glaring circle of spotlight that is concentrated on me. Baby pink, I think, good color; I'm learning. I am sitting on a high stool, my left foot propped up on a rung, my guitar securely balanced on my knee. My hand is poised midair for a moment. I can hear the silence all around me. I can hear them waiting. I swore I would never play "Blues for Linda Ann" again, but that's what they expect tonight. That's what they want from me. So I go into the familiar opening measures. I cannot understand him. I cannot condone him. I cannot even forgive him. But the pain in his music is real, whatever caused it, and I am feeling his pain now. This is for you, Silk Garcia. This is for you.

1

I almost went to Jeffrey Breslow's that afternoon. Or, if it hadn't been so cold, we might have stayed on the corner, talking, for an extra five minutes. Either way, I would have missed Big Ray Bronson and I don't think my mother ever would have said a word.

"Come on over, Lin."

Jeffrey and I were on the corner of Lloyd Hill and High Street, where we separated on the way home from school. I hesitated, because I liked sitting around his big, comfortable living room, with his nutty mother feeding us hot chocolate and things. And I still sometimes had that sad feeling, left over from when I was little, about coming home to an empty apartment.

"No, I can't," I said. "I've got to practice."

His mittened hand played with the string from my hood. "Well, can I come over and listen?" he asked.

I smiled and shook my head. Whenever Jeff came over to hear my guitar practice, to do homework, whatever, he would talk and talk. He could get very wound up, analyzing me, himself, the town of North Bay, the personality of the bird, biological breakthroughs, the geological foundation of Long Island. . . . Because of

Jeff, I've become very aware of a lot of things most people don't see. But the afternoon would go by, and I'd get nothing done.

He was jiggling from one foot to the other with the cold. "When do you start at G.I., Linny?" G.I. was the Guitar Institute.

"Next Tuesday, and I really have to be good."

"You're being neurotic again," he said. "You don't need to impress anyone; you're just taking classes. Anyway, you *are* good. So come on over and see the baby parakeets."

Jeff was into genetics and breeding parakeets. His world was dominant and recessive genes, and while other kids dreamed of scoring the winning goal or something, he dreamed of producing the first red parakeet. These, he explained, were his fatal flaws: aggressive intelligence and basic scrawniness in a football town. My fatal flaws were living in an apartment over a store and, Jeff thought, having my confidence wrecked by the taboo about my father. We weren't part of the "in" crowd. Jeff had high school subdivisions down pat, just like parakeet color groups.

"I'll come see the babies soon," I said. "Not today."

"Okay. See you tomorrow."

"See you."

Jeff started up the hill. I shifted my books so that I could get my other hand into my jacket pocket. The wind whipped my hair and I walked fast, head down. There was no snow left on the ground. The lawns I passed looked ragged, and the rhododendron leaves were curled up into miserable slivers. Even the rich part of town looked bleak at the end of January.

Then came Main Street, with sidewalks and stores and the Long Island Railroad station. I lived over Varian's Gifts and Imports. The window was full of ceramic tigers, dogs and Moroccan rugs. I usually checked it out

4

to see if there was anything new, but today it was too cold, so I rushed into the building doorway.

I went up the narrow stairs, like always, and opened the door like always, and then stopped in surprise. My mother was supposed to be at work, but I was hearing her voice.

"Like what, for instance?" she said.

"There's not much . . ." A man's voice, very deep.

A short, nasty laugh from Mom. "I wouldn't think so."

Looking down the hall, I could see the back of his head over the couch. Large head, black, nappy hair, thick brown neck.

". . . some clothes and records," he said. "The amplifier's a good one. It should be worth something."

"I don't want it."

"Jeannie, it's got to be worth close to a thousand."

"Listen, I'll bet he owed you a hell of a lot more than that."

"He'd have wanted to leave something for the kid," he said. "You could sell it or . . ."

"Do you want to hear something funny? She plays the guitar. How lucky can I get?"

They were talking about me; "the kid" was me! I became acutely aware of standing there, eavesdropping.

"How's she doing?"

"Fine. She's a good kid, doing okay in school. She's fifteen now. . . ." I couldn't believe the note of approval. That wasn't the message I had been getting from Mom.

"Fifteen. Jesus, what a lot of years gone by."

A long silence. "Anyway," my mother said, "keep everything or sell it or whatever. I don't want it."

"Jeannie, Jeannie, I didn't come here looking to hurt you."

"I know."

"I guess I shouldn't have come. I just felt like I should, you know?"

"I know. It's good to see you. Really. It's just that . . ." Mom's voice was choking off. "Anyway, it's all over for him."

"Yeah," he said. A sigh. "Well, I'm gigging over in Jersey tonight, so . . ."

The couch creaked as they stood up. As quietly as I could, I backed up a few steps and partly closed the door. Then I rattled my keys and the doorknob to make a racket and a big show of opening the door.

My mother was standing in the hall, facing me, and she looked terrible. Her eyes were red and puffy, and the end of her nose was red. I was surprised to see that she had been crying.

"Jesus," the man whispered, "it's like seeing a ghost!"

He was staring at me. He was a huge black man who was shoehorned into a pale gray suit. Most of his face was beard.

"Her eyes, Jeannie! It's Silk all over again." He seemed so emotional, but my mother's face was stone cold. So this was about my father. I felt a little rush of excitement.

"Linda," Mom said, "this is Mr. Bronson, a friend of your father's."

"Hi," I said. This man had all kinds of feelings showing on his face. It was awkward.

"Linda, I am glad to see you," he said. He swept me into a bear hug, and my arms dangled at my sides. Then he was getting into his coat and buttoning up and they were saying things like, "Keep in touch" and "Take care of yourself, Jeannie," and he was going. I felt as if I were watching the scene in a movie, and it was going by too fast. I wanted to rerun the last sequence, to sit down on the couch with this man, to talk about my father. It was slipping away.

6

"Do I look that much like him?" I asked.

"Dead ringer," he said. And he was gone.

I followed Mom through the living room into our bedroom. She went directly to the mirror and concentrated on fixing the wisps of blond hair that had escaped.

"What was that all about?" I asked.

"Your father's dead," she said. She was undoing the French twist and starting all over. Bobby pins were sticking out of her clenched teeth. "That was Big Ray Bronson; he plays the trumpet; he was with your father for years. He came to tell me."

Not yet, I thought. I had been waiting all this time for some sign from him and now there would be nothing. I crumpled.

"What happened to him?"

"Hepatitis, I think."

"You think? How can you think and not know?" My voice rose.

"Well, hepatitis and complications."

"When? What did that man say? What kind of complications?"

"Look, Linda, there's nothing else to say about it." Our eyes met in the mirror. "He died last week. That's all."

"What about the funeral or—?"

"It's all over," she said. "Oh, come on, you never even knew him. . . . I have to get back to work."

"What for? It's late."

"I have to help close up," she said. Every hair was now meticulously in place, and she was working on her lips. Lip liner first, then lipstick, then gloss. Super neat. I couldn't believe her.

"My God," I yelled, "he was my father!"

"Oh, stop it," she said. "Look, I'm sorry if you're upset, but this has nothing to do with us."

"You were crying," I said. "You look awful."

"All right, I was crying. I was married to the man once." She headed back into the living room and I followed. "I have to go," she said. "Get some chopped meat out of the freezer and—"

"So you must have cared."

She turned and gave me a long look. "I wasn't crying for him. I was crying for me. So let it go, all right?" She was in her coat and tying the belt. "I'll be home around six."

"Can't you wait a minute? Can't you tell me what the man said?"

"Nothing. He said nothing. Just what I told you."

"Well, where did he die?"

"Beth Israel."

"Beth Israel?"

"That hospital down in the twenties, in the city."

"New York? He was in New York all this time?" Good God; just a few miles away!

"I don't know. . . . Look, we're taking inventory. I have to get back."

"Was that man with him?"

"Will you stop bugging me and just leave me alone!" And she was out the door, fast, trailing fumes of hairspray.

That was the way it always ended when I was little. I'd probe and probe and she would give me calm nonanswers, as if she were wrapped in a cocoon. Then finally it would get to her, and she would explode. I hadn't asked her about him in years.

Antonio Garcia, also known as "Silk" Garcia. Why Silk? Now I would never know. I was surprised by the amount of pain that flooded me. How can you feel the loss of someone who was never in your life?

I wandered back into the bedroom. Mom's lipstick and bobby pins were scattered on the dresser. I leaned

8

over until my face was just inches from the mirror. "Jesus," Bronson had said, "it's like seeing a ghost." I pushed my long hair back and studied my reflection. I tried to find Silk Garcia, but I could only see myself. Large gray eyes. ("Your best feature. You should always make the most of your best feature. Why don't you use some mascara?" Mom sometimes sounded like a back issue of *Vogue*.) Olive skin. High cheekbones. Dark straight eyebrows. ("You should tweeze them and arch them a little. I'll do it for you," Mom said.) A widow's peak and straight brown hair. I tried to see a man with my face, a man with large gray eyes. So I was Silk Garcia's double. I wonder, I thought if that's why Mom is always trying to correct my face. That was unfair; she was forever doing something to her face, too. She was in her fashion thing. Poor Mom. She stood around all day at the boutique on the Miracle Mile and came home with swollen ankles.

I certainly didn't look like Mom or any of the other Quinns. Grandma and Mom and Aunt Katherine were fair, blue-eyed, softly rounded. When Mom first brought me back to Long Island, we lived in Grandma's house on Sandbar Road. There was a picture of Mom on the mantel. She was five; curly blond hair, a rather smug, dimpled smile, ruffled blue dress, a gold heart locket around her neck. At five, I was all angles and bones, and I knew I was an odd bird, dropped by the cuckoo.

There were conversations I overheard in the night, half asleep.

"You could certainly go back to your maiden name," Grandma said. "Millions of women do, you know. There's no reason why . . ."

"I just happen to have a child named Garcia." My mother's voice, tired and monotone.

"Well, naturally, you'd change hers, too. Linda Quinn."

9

"Ma, it's not that easy. Legally, she . . ."

Mom worked and Grandma watched over me. I heard her talking to Aunt Katherine. "She's such a restless little thing, not at all like Jeannie was," and, "Honestly, Katherine, I never expected to have to raise a second family at my age."

Grandma's house was small and wood-shingled, with a tiny front yard where she grew marigolds every summer. The houses on Sandbar Road were close together and painstakingly maintained to ward off shabbiness, though there were some renegades with peeling paint or broken porch steps. Grandma's house was five streets away from the lushly landscaped world of Lloyd Hill where Jeffrey Breslow lived and a short walk away from the apartments on Main Street near the railroad station. It must have been hard for Mom to come back to the little ruffled bedroom where she had grown up. Grandma didn't say much, but she looked at her with a kind of outraged disappointment. I think's that's why Mom moved to the apartment over Varian's.

The guitar and record came when I was seven, just before Mom and I moved.

"What kind of thing is that to send to a little girl?" Grandma said. I had opened the package, tearing the brown wrapping. It was addressed to Miss Linda Garcia. There was a full-sized guitar and a record. No note, no return address. The postmark was St. Louis. We knew it was from my father, because the record featured Silk Garcia on guitar. It was on the Royal Roost label. One side was "Zigzag," the flip side was "Blues for Linda Ann." I thought that was really fantastic, just terrific, I mean, having my name on a real record!

"What are you supposed to do with a guitar?" Grandma asked. "You'd think he could have sent the money."

"I don't know." Mom, expressionless.

10

"Well, if he's making records, you'd think he could help out. . . . I can tell you, it just eats me up to think of all the chances you threw away—"

"Ma, please, let's not . . ."

I was just entering second grade, and I brought the record in for Show and Tell. I said that my father was a professional musician and wrote songs just for me. The kids asked about the words, and I had to say there were no words, just music. But everyone could see my name right there.

I hardly touched the guitar then. I didn't even know how to tune it. It wasn't until a couple of years later that it became important to me.

The North Bay school system gave free music lessons in band and orchestra instruments to fourth graders. At the end of third grade, the music teacher, Miss Cornell, checked us out to make recommendations, so that a kid with braces wouldn't be playing trumpet, for instance. And we were all given a little test of listening to some notes and scales on the piano and then humming them. When my turn came, Miss Cornell really perked up. It seemed that I had perfect pitch. She sent a note home with me that afternoon, telling Mom that I showed signs of special talent and should definitely participate in the music program. I felt pretty good about that. This was the first time in my school career that I felt outstanding in any way, so I couldn't wait for Mom to come home from work to show her the note. I was hopping up and down when I gave it to her; I watched her face eagerly while she read it.

She crumpled the note with a look of distaste. Her voice was tight. "There's no way we can afford to buy some instrument."

"But Mommy, kids rent—"

"Or rent one. Those things cost a lot."

"Mommy," I wailed.

"They just want kids playing something to fill up their bands. Don't make a big thing out of it."

"But she said I had special talent. I was the only one that had *special* talent."

She studied me with—I don't know—apprehension, maybe, and her voice became shrill. "No. That's all. No!"

She hadn't even tried to get an instrument for me. I knew it had something to do with my father and from then on, I was on his side, whoever he was.

I was shy in third grade, especially with grown-ups, and it took courage to talk to Mr. Buccalati. Mr. Buccalati came to the elementary school from the junior high twice a week to teach string instruments. I waited outside his room, listening to the agonized shrieks of Freddy Boyle's violin. When Freddy left, I plunged in.

"Mr. Buccalati," I said desperately.

"Yes?"

"I'm Linda Garcia. I'm supposed to take lessons with you next year."

"Oh?"

"I mean, I want to, but my mother can't get me a regular instrument but I have a guitar—I mean, that *is* a string instrument, isn't it, and I was wondering . . ." I waited breathlessly.

He looked at me curiously. He looked young, for a teacher, and friendly. "We teach band and orchestra instruments. You know that, don't you?"

"Yes."

"And I teach in groups of three. No private lessons. I'm sorry, I just wouldn't have the time."

I mumbled something and looked at the floor. Gray linoleum with white specks.

"Oh, what the hell," he said. "Half the children here drop out anyway." He studied me. "Are you going to be serious about this?"

12

"Oh, yes!" Breathlessly.

"You know, my major was classical guitar. Do you have any idea how hard it is?"

"No."

"Well, it is. You might be too young . . ."

"Oh no, I won't be too young, Mr. Buccalati."

"All right, let's give it a try and see what happens."

I had lessons with Joseph Buccalati once a week for a year, and it was insanely hard. He took me through Carulli studies and Segovia scales and pushed my nine-year-old fingers further than they could go. I practiced like a demon, partly for his "Excellent!" and partly because it seemed to bug Mom. I cultivated long, rounded nails on my right hand, my picking hand. I kept the nails on my left hand trimmed short and proudly watched the calluses form on my fingertips. The marks of a guitarist. I was running through Beatles things and Fleetwood Mac and the early Renaissance pieces that Joseph Buccalati loved. And sometimes I tried to play along with my father's record.

I still had the record, worn now from repeated playing. "Zigzag," on electric guitar, was fast and flashy; Silk Garcia was obviously a virtuoso. "Blues for Linda Ann," on acoustic, was something else.

I turned on the phonograph and curled up on my bed, hugging my knees. I listened to it and thought about his being dead and shivered as his message came through to me again. It started very slowly, a dark sound of Spain, heavy on the vibrato. Then, imperceptibly, the Spanish wail turned into black blues. An aching melody, full of regrets. Broken rhythms. Wild dissonances. And an abrupt end. He must have loved me to have felt all that pain for Linda Ann.

2

I elbowed my way into the high school cafeteria, through the smell of greasy hamburgers and a haze of noise. Lunch was the only period I had with Jeffrey. He was taking Honors Calculus and Advanced Placement Bio and my schedule was just the ordinary required sophomore things. Jeff always saved a chair for me, which was a lot more valiant than it sounds. There was an excess of tables and an undersupply of chairs, so getting a chair in the first place and then trying to hold on to it was a hassle. I've seen more fights break out over chairs.

I looked for Jeff in the corner near the beverage counter. The different groups flocked to their regular places. On the left, two tables of the black kids from the Cliff Homes projects. On the far side, the performing arts group, the ones in all the plays. The jocks hung together. So did the potheads. Holding court in the center, the glittering top strata of North Bay High School, Michael Harrison and that crowd. Michael Harrison was in Technicolor while everybody else was in black and white. Sandy hair flecked with sunshine, a golden tan from Bermuda or wherever people who live in Ocean

Point go for Christmas vacation. The Michael Harrison crowd, Jeff said, had perfect smiles and no fatal flaws. Jeff meant that as a put-down, as if they were uninteresting. I thought they were lucky.

I found Jeff, and he automatically pushed part of his lunch across the table to me. There was a huge slab of French bread with liverwurst and a handful of carrots and an apple. Jeff's mother wanted him to gain weight, so she insisted on giving him an overstuffed bag with triple portions of everything. I had been saving my lunch money. That and baby-sitting for my Aunt Katherine were going to pay for the Guitar Institute. Anyway, I loved Mrs. Breslow's cold cuts.

"So . . ." I said between bites, "this Big Ray Bronson looked really upset. 'It's Silk all over again.' Isn't that strange?"

"No. Why shouldn't you look like your father?"

"And I've never even seen a picture of him. Nothing. No letters. No contact. I've never heard of any other divorced father so totally cancelled out."

"Maybe you're illegitimate," Jeff said. "Maybe it was a one-night stand."

"No, they were together until I was two, I know that much. Sometimes I think I remember him."

"Do you?"

"Just vague things. I don't know if I really remember or if it's something I've dreamed."

"Like what?"

"Well, riding along on his shoulders and ducking under the awnings and laughing. And another thing. Hanging on to his arm with both hands and the smell of gasoline and a lot of loud voices."

"Is that all?"

"That's all."

"Things like that don't tell you anything," Jeff said.

"I tried to get in touch with him a few times. I tried

to call Royal Roost, you know, the label on his record, but I guess they weren't in business anymore. And once I called St. Louis Information to see if they had a listing for him."

"Why St. Louis?"

"I thought he might be there. Because of the postmark on the package. Anyway, I called all the Antonio Garcias—there were five—and they didn't know what I was talking about. Mom flipped out when she saw the bill. You know, I was always sure, just positive, he'd get in touch with me sometime. But now . . ."

Amy Buren, all braces, and Mark Stimson brushed past our table, so intertwined that Mark was having trouble balancing his tray. I leaned away and kept a wary eye on his grape juice. Once I was rushing down to my locker during third period and I almost tripped over Amy and Mark locked together on the stairs. I wondered if they ever went to classes.

"The thing is," I said, "my mother gives me the feeling that there was something about him . . . something about me . . . like I have the mark of Dracula."

"Hey, Linny—"

"You know those movies where someone looks perfectly normal, but suddenly hair starts growing on his face and—"

"Dracula's a vampire, not a werewolf. Try not to be a fuzzy thinker."

"So now he's dead and I'll never know. I look just like him, I even play the same instrument. How far can heredity go, Jeff?"

"Assume an ear for music is hereditary, okay? So is manual dexterity. Obviously, eye color, features. You're talking about the purely physical. Your instrument turned out to be the guitar because that's what you had available. That's all. As a matter of fact, you'd have been better off with the violin or flute."

"I really have to know about him."

"Okay, Linda," Jeff said. "If you think you have to, then you do."

"I have to talk to this Big Ray Bronson."

"How do you spell it, *s-e-n* or *s-o-n?*"

"I don't know."

"Well, it can't be that hard to find the guy." Jeff stood up and neatly gathered the litter into the brown paper bag. "Come over this afternoon, and I'll help you think of something."

"You take Manhattan and I'll take Queens."

Jeffrey and I were sitting cross-legged on the orange shag carpeting in his living room, surrounded by telephone books. The Breslows had moved from New York City a little less than a year ago and had special-ordered Manhattan, Queens and Brooklyn telephone directories. All we had at my house was the Nassau County book and the local North Bay directory. The Quinns went back three generations in North Bay.

I ran my finger down the column of Bronsons in Manhattan. No Ray. No Raymond. Then I tried the Bronsens. I could hear Mrs. Breslow upstairs, talking to Jeff's little brother, Arnold.

"Arnold, go out and play."

"But, Mom, it's fifteen degrees!"

"That doesn't matter—it's very sunny and you can put on your snow jacket. . . ."

"Mom, I want to do my stamps."

"Well, get some fresh air first; we moved all the way out here from the city, so take advantage of the fresh—"

"Mom, it's freezing out there!"

I could hear Mrs. Breslow coming down the stairs and then she did her routine outside the living room. Whenever Jeff and I were alone in a room, she would stop and cough and give us lots of warning before she came in. It was weird. She must have thought we were having some kind of orgy. I guess it was nice of her to try to give us some privacy, but Jeff and I just talked a lot, so it was embarrassing.

"Well, Linda," she said, coming in after her pregnant pause, "you're looking very pretty today. How've you been?"

"Fine, thanks, Mrs. Breslow."

She gave me a big toothy smile, and I smiled back. Most of the time she overdid the welcome, I guess because Jeff didn't have that many friends to bring home.

"Well, what are you kids doing?"

"Looking through the telephone books, Mom," Jeff said.

"Oh, that's very nice," she said, smiling at us. "Is that a project for school?"

"Yes, Mom," Jeff said.

"Sounds interesting," she said and waited for a while, hoping to be included, I think. Then she wandered out.

"Would you kids like some pastry? I have some from Eclair," Mrs. Breslow called from the kitchen.

"Yes, I'll be right there," Jeff said.

"Mmmmm, Eclair," I said.

"My mother still gets everything from the city. Bread from Zabar's etcetera, etcetera."

"Isn't that a lot of trouble?"

"Yeah. She misses the city a lot."

"Was it your father who wanted to move to North Bay?"

"Hell, no! He hates commuting. We barely see him, and he's always worn out."

"Then why . . .?"

"Obviously, 'for the sake of the children.' "

"I can't imagine living anywhere but here," I said.

"Do you know what makes the city so great for kids?

18

Transportation. Public transportation. Buses. Subways. Cabs. The whole world is yours."

"You'll get used to North Bay, Jeff," I said. "Honestly, the kids'll get friendlier after a while and—"

"North Bay is the center of Jockdom."

"And the beaches are beautiful. Wait until summer."

"I'd like to be going to the Bronx High School of Science, then I'd *enjoy* school."

"Why didn't your mother let you go there?"

"I would have had to travel all the way up to the Bronx from Fifty-fifth Street. She was afraid I'd get mugged. Haven't you noticed, my mother hovers."

I didn't think she hovered exactly; she just didn't seem to have much else to do but concentrate on Jeffrey and Arnold.

If you were going to pick two exactly opposite mothers, Mrs. Breslow and Mom would have to be it. Mrs. Breslow was very vivacious and Mom was so tired; half the time she was like a zombie. Saleswomen have to stand around all day and it was hard on her. Jeff's mother dressed kind of trendy—bright colors, different things all the time. Mom wore a few really good things in beiges and black, and she took excellent care of them, trying to make them last longer. I think she cared a lot about setting herself apart from the welfare people who lived in our building. Mrs. B. was easygoing about things that would make Mom hit the ceiling. She once made a speech to Jeff that went something like this: "I'm sure you'll try pot sometime in high school, so I'd be happier if you and your friends did it right here, at home, and not on some street corner someplace." That shook Jeff because he hadn't been planning to try pot or anything else. It would be nice if Mrs. B. stopped expecting un-Jeff-like things from him. On that same subject, Mom went so far overboard the other way that it was unbelievable.

19

Jeff flicked the telephone book shut. "That does it for Queens and Brooklyn. Anything in Manhattan?"

"Nothing." I felt discouraged. "Nothing in Nassau, either."

"Don't worry, we'll find him."

Jeff went into the kitchen and brought back a plate of tiny cream puffs. Then he got busy on the phone. I was so grateful for Jeff. I could never have coped with asking the information operator to check that many listings. He patiently requested Westchester Information and Staten Island and the Bronx and then Suffolk and very politely asked them to check both spellings.

"Yes, *s-e-n* or *s-o-n*. Thank you very much. Ray or maybe Raymond or just *R*. Yes, thank you. . . ."

The cream puffs had mocha icing and the insides had an incredibly light, real vanilla taste. I ate and watched Jeff's face for a sign of good news.

"Lin, nothing at all. He might have an unlisted number."

"I thought it would be easy. I thought it would be in the Manhattan book, first try."

"It would be a lot easier if you could ask your mother."

"I can't."

"How about your Aunt Katherine?"

"I don't think my Aunt Katherine would know anything about him. I could ask her, though." She lived just a few blocks away from us and was easy to talk to.

"Any other ideas?" Jeff said.

"Well, Bronson said something about gigging in New Jersey that night. . . ."

"Lin, do you know how many clubs there must be in the entire state of New Jersey? And it might not even be a club. He might be working weddings or bar mitzvahs."

"Oh, no, Jeff, I think he'd be beyond that. My mother said he was with my father for years."

20

"I'll think of something, don't worry. . . . There's vanilla cream on your chin, no, on the left. . . . Come help me do the birds."

We went into the Bird Room. The Breslows used to call it the Plant Room until the birds took over. Actually, it was an enclosed porch. The first time I was there, it was really pretty. There were trailing plants hanging from the ceiling and some big plants in the corners, avocados and philodendrons, and pots of begonias scattered around. There was a wrought-iron couch, some chairs and a red brick floor. It had looked like an indoor garden. And then Jeff acquired Sam and the Breslows discovered that free-flying parakeets behave like locusts and destroy greenery. Most of the plants had been moved out and now there were only a few forlorn ones left. There were dry leaves, bits of bark, tiny feathers and some droppings scattered on the brick floor. One terrific thing about Mrs. Breslow was that she was tolerant of the birds.

Sam swooped down on my head as we entered the room, a fluff of lilac and gray. I automatically extended my finger for him to perch on and brought him down to my shoulder. I really did like Sam, but not enough to risk bird droppings in my hair. Sam was the first of the birds, from an aviary farther out on the island. He was a Violet with a pink cast that Jeff said was unusual. He discovered that no one had ever been able to breed red tones, so, Jeff being Jeff, was going to try. To start with, he was trying to establish a strain of Violets with a deeper pink cast. Now there were four adults plus Jeff's first clutch in the nest box.

"Could I see the babies?" I asked.

"Just for a minute." Jeff slid out the back of the nest box. The mother was inside, and I could barely see two of the four infants. They looked awkward, helpless and touching in their ugliness. Birds without feathers are not cute.

"How old are they now?"

"The oldest is five days. They don't all hatch at the same time." He carefully closed the box.

"When do their feathers come in?"

"The down should start to show soon. They sprout tail feathers at about two weeks. At three weeks, the breast feathers start to open."

"Oh, Jeff, I hope you get a Red."

He laughed. "The most I can hope for at this point is a deeper pink tone. Actually, a Red would be the result of a mutation. It might be impossible."

"Don't say impossible. Difficult."

"Okay, Lin. How about unlikely?"

Jeff talked for a while about inbreeding and cross-breeding and sex-linked chromosomes. Hanging around with Jeff had taught me more about parakeets than I ever wanted to know. Sam flew off my shoulder and down the length of the room.

"I was lucky. I think Sam's turning out to be a terrific father." Jeff was sweeping up. "You know, they need both the mother and father to feed them. You saw the hen in the nest box. She stays there to keep warm, and Sam feeds her. Then, when the feathers come in, she leaves the box and gets some rest, and both parents take turns feeding the babies. I was lucky because sometimes tame birds don't make such great parents."

What about humans, I thought. Why couldn't my father make it as a parent?

It was getting to be late afternoon, still daylight, but on the verge of evening. The sun was covered by clouds, and the light coming through the windows was cold and gray. I watched Sam circle the room and land on Jeff.

"I thought of something," Jeff said slowly.

"What?"

"I don't know if . . . You said your father died at Beth Israel."

"Right."

"My cousin Marvin is an intern at Beth Israel. He could probably poke around and check records, maybe find out things like an address or who claimed the—uh—body."

"Please ask him."

"I was just wondering if you really want to—"

"Yes, I want to know."

"Maybe your mother has a good reason for—"

"Jeff, whatever it is, I want to know."

"Even if it's something bad?"

"Whatever happened was between my mother and father, not me. It's crazy not to let me know anything about my own father."

"I guess that's true."

"So ask your cousin, all right?"

"All right."

"Please ask him as soon as you can."

"All right, I will."

"Give him my number, okay, and tell him to call before six, before Mom gets home. Maybe you'd better not say I'm his daughter; that would seem kind of strange. Just say I'm a distant relative."

"I'll talk to him. His name is Marvin Breslow. . . . Can you get me some grit, Linda?"

I held the container of grit and watched Jeff mix little bits of it into the seed cups.

"Well," he said, "that should about do it for Bird Land."

"There really was a place called Birdland once," I said.

"You mean the World of Birds at the Bronx Zoo? It's a fantastic—"

"No, Birdland was a jazz nightclub in the city, years ago. It was named for Charlie 'Bird' Parker and—"

"Who?" Jeff asked. The disappointing thought about Jeff was that he knew nothing about music.

"He played the sax. Anyway, I read about it in one of the history of jazz books at the library." I had been looking through a lot of those books, and I never found the name of Silk Garcia in any of them. "Charlie Parker was called 'Bird,' and they were going to carry the bird theme all the way through in his honor. They were going to have cages of finches, hundreds of finches of all colors, suspended from the ceiling. Wouldn't that be fantastic, having a place like that in honor of your nickname?"

"Finches! Finches are the most timid of birds, not at all adaptable to captivity! And can you imagine having all that smoke and noise rise up to the cages?"

"Oh, Jeff, they probably didn't even have the finches."

"I hope not. First of all, birds have to have their regular periods of light and dark, and a place like that would be lit up all night. Can't you just see them replacing hundreds of dead finches every week? Dying of fright and—"

"It was probably just an idea. I don't think they had live birds. . . ." I watched Sam on Jeff's shoulder, nibbling at his neck, and I felt guilty. I hadn't thought of the birds at all. I had been thinking of how absolutely cool it would be for a club to be named after me. Lindaland. Actually, that didn't sound so great; it would be better to have a nickname. . . .

"How can people be so dense, using live birds for decoration!"

"Anyway, it was a great place. People like Dizzy Gillespie and George Shearing played there. Ever hear of 'Lullaby of Birdland'? People crowded in every night to hear the music and . . ."

I could see that Jeff wasn't listening. I was sure he was still thinking about the finches and wanting to save them. I drifted off into more thoughts of Lindaland.

24

"Presenting, on guitar . . . Miss Linda Garcia!" The nice thing about Jeff and me was that we never stepped on each other's fantasies.

I had a dream that night. I was on a flying trapeze, high above the circus floor, wearing lavender spangles and smiling. Far across the void was my partner, in matching spangled tights, a man with my face. His arms were outstretched, ready to catch me. I was all smiles and confidence as I hurtled through the air, the crowd cheering. My hands were out, ready to grasp my partner's. But he was not reaching for me! He was just sitting on the bar, swinging absentmindedly! I screamed for him, but he just sat there, humming. I was falling into blackness. Falling. Falling. I woke up, my body still falling. I listened to my mother breathing in her sleep in the twin bed across the room. I lay very, very still, for a long time, before I could go back to sleep.

3

It had to be pouring on my first day at the Guitar Institute. Going into a new situation like that and wondering if I'd measure up made me uncomfortable, so I thought I'd at least look as nice as possible. I was wearing new jeans and my favorite top, a white cowl-necked sweater, and I had planned to wear a really nice pair of clogs. I had washed my hair and used Mom's blow-dryer for an hour the night before to get the ends to curl up. But it was raining, and by the time I got home from school my hair was hanging in wet strands. I looked out of the window in disgust. The rain was coming down in sheets so I'd have to wear my old raincoat and, even worse, the old clunky rain boots which made my feet look enormous. I didn't even have time to fix my hair, because I'd miss the bus. I grabbed the guitar and an umbrella and ran down the stairs, feeling messy and rushed.

The Guitar Institute was in a vacant elementary school in the next town. The bus stop was right near my house, near the railroad station, but the bus ran only once an hour and I had to hurry home from school to make it, without a minute to spare. The bad part about the trip was that the Guitar Institute was up a hill, five blocks from where the bus left me off. It was awful in the rain. My guitar case was dripping water, and I worried about whether any of it was getting in. It was hard to hold the umbrella steady—the wind kept blowing under it.

Joseph Buccalati had told me about G.I. We had been talking about getting more into jazz and rock.

"Look," Joe said, "I'm strictly a Renaissance man, and if you want to get into this other stuff, you should check out G.I. I know you can't swing private lessons, but they have some kind of state grant, and I hear they give good group classes."

Their catalogue was wonderful! They had classes in classical, flamenco, jazz, folk, rock, anything you could ever want, and someday I'd like to go every day. For now, I picked two classes for Tuesday afternoons.

Advanced Improv 1: Advanced improvisation in major and minor keys . . .

I also wanted to take something in arranging and I picked Arranging, Intermediate 2 because it would be on the same day.

Arranging, Intermediate 2: Arrangements using various fretboard positions. Arrangements for two or more guitars . . .

I talked to Joe again before I signed up.

"Do you think I'm ready for it? I mean, Advanced Improv?"

"You can do it. One of these days you're going to start believing in yourself, and you're going to be a holy terror. And don't forget to stop by and let me know how you're doing."

I didn't feel like a holy terror today. Here I was, walking in all alone, nervous about being behind everyone else in the class, strands of wet hair hanging along my cheeks. It wasn't a terrific entrance.

There was a long, narrow hall and a small group of people sitting on the floor near the main door. They looked up at me when I came in.

"Hello." An auburn-haired boy.

"Hello," I said.

"Have a nice swim?" he said with a big grin.

"You'd better get a towel or something; they have some in the lounge." From a girl wearing a yellow Guitar Institute T-shirt.

"Well, my class starts at three-thirty, I—"

"Don't worry, you're early, and nothing starts on time around here, anyway," she said. "You're new, aren't you? Do you know where the lounge is?"

"No, I don't."

"Come on, I'll show you around." She unwound from the floor, long, lanky, in very faded, patched jeans. "Oh, I'm Irene. This is Tommy, Susan, Caroline and . . ." A lot of names that I'd have to sort out later.

"Hi, I'm Linda Garcia." There was a chorus of hi's. I was glad these kids seemed so friendly. At North Bay High, if people didn't know each other, they just looked each other over and didn't say anything.

"Come on," said Irene, and I followed her down the hall. The lounge was really an old kitchen crowded with some desks and chairs and a terrible-looking couch— mud brown with some springs sticking out. Irene handed me a roll of paper towels and watched while I dried my face and tried to mop up my hair.

"You must be freezing," she said. "Do you want some tea or coffee?"

"Tea would be great, thanks."

"Did anyone show you around or anything?"

28

"Well, no."

"Okay. Here are tea bags and instant coffee—help yourself anytime, and once in a while put some change in this jar so they can buy new stuff." She was boiling the water and getting paper cups. "You can keep things in the refrigerator; do you take Saturday classes?"

"No, just Tuesday afternoons."

"Saturday people usually keep their lunches here. Or you can bring something for between classes. I'm a yogurt freak. . . ."

The tea was ready and I took a sip. It was very hot and burned my tongue.

"How long have you been coming here?" I said.

"Let's see. Three years. Damn, this is hot!" She put her cup down. "Oh, about the Xerox. If you need to copy sheet music for class, that's free, and if it's for your own use, that's a dime for each copy, in the jar over there." A glass jar, labeled XEROX, half full of change. That would be ripped off in about five minutes at North Bay High School.

"What are you taking?"

"Advanced Improvisation and Arranging, Intermediate 2."

"Advanced Improv? You must be good. Tommy, you know, in the hall, is in that. I have Chamber Ensemble this afternoon and a whole slew of things on Saturday. . . . We'd better go. Are you feeling better?"

"Oh, yes. Thanks a lot."

Classes were about to start and the hall was busier and noisier. Irene swung along and waved here and there. She left me at Room 2.

Advanced Improvisation had only five people, including Tommy, the redhead from the hall. The class turned out to be hard, but I thought I was holding my own. Tommy sat next to me and talked to me a little, and I started to feel very comfortable.

29

There was a break before my next class, and I waited in the hall. There were groups of people sitting around on the floor, playing different things right next to each other. Villa-Lobos and the Rolling Stones. All different kinds of music, a sprinkling of middle-aged people, a couple of kids that looked about ten, many in their teens and twenties. Some long-haired hippie-looking guys, some folk-singer girls—sincere-looking with no makeup and plain hair severely pulled back.

A big bulletin board was on the wall, crowded with notices, and I started reading them. "Yamaha amplifier for sale, call Bill. . . . Early Music Consort appearing on . . . Bass guitarist needed for . . . Blue Grass Festival on . . . For Sale: Favila guitar . . . American Federation of Musicians. . . ." I stopped short. How obvious, why hadn't I thought of it before! The musicians' union, of course! I could surely get in touch with Big Ray Bronson through the union. He had to be a member! I'd call first chance tomorrow.

I was feeling very pleased with myself when I went into Room 8 for Arranging. Seven people in the class, including me. A very serious-looking girl of maybe twelve, a woman in her thirties, three college-aged boys and . . . Michael Harrison! *The* Michael Harrison. I said "hi" to him and he said "hi" back. He gave me a friendly, kind of blank look, and I realized he had no idea who I was. The teacher was late and we all sat around, tuning our guitars, waiting.

Pat Calhoun burst into the room. He had the kind of looks my grandmother calls "Black Irish": black hair, dark eyes, very fair skin.

"Sorry, I got tied up," Pat said. "I'll give you extra time at the end, okay?"

Extra time at the end. That meant I'd miss the five-thirty bus and have to wait around until six-thirty. I hated the idea of going back down that hill in the rain.

"Okay, why don't we just go around and have each of you play something you've been doing, just so I know where you are."

I was second, and I picked a Fleetwood Mac number and put a lot of extra doodles in it.

"That's pretty good," Pat said. "Is that extra stuff your own?"

"Yes."

"Good. Very nice."

That really set me up. It was a good class. He showed us different picks and gave us an assignment for the next week, working out some complicated bass runs. He gave us a lot of extra time, and I would have enjoyed it if I hadn't been thinking about getting home. Michael Harrison, I thought, could I ask him for a ride? I didn't want to; I didn't even know him, but that hill. . . . It was dark and still raining and probably freezing by now. I rushed out after him when we left the class.

"I was wondering, could I have a ride back to North Bay with you? I mean, if you have a ride?"

"North Bay?" he said. "Yeah. Sure."

He looked at me, puzzled, and I could feel my face getting warm. He didn't even know that I went to the same high school. There's nothing like feeling anonymous.

"My name's Linda Garcia. I go to North Bay High, too."

"I thought you looked familiar."

"Is anyone picking you up? Would they mind . . .?"

"I've got my car right outside."

I really felt stupid. He was a junior; obviously he was old enough to have a license. And of course Michael Harrison would have his own car.

The windshield wipers were going triple time as we drove along Shoreview Road to the Boulevard. He was concentrating on the road. I had never seen him close up

31

before. His profile was perfect, right down to long eye-lashes. He looked sun-drenched. He belonged in a California surfing movie, not in a rainy Long Island night.

"You can really play that thing," he said.

"Thanks."

"Pat was impressed. So was I."

"Well, I've been working at it for a long time."

"You really work at it, huh?"

"Well, yes."

"You're serious about it?"

"I guess so."

"What would you want to do?" he asked.

"I don't know. Play lead guitar, I guess." I thought I sounded pretty dumb, and I wished I had said something more definite. What do I want to do? Play a fantastic guitar, even better than Silk Garcia, sing, be beautiful, be a star. That's not the thing to say to a stranger. Or a friend either, for that matter, or anybody.

I should say something else, I thought. He seemed nice. Perfectly human. The trouble was I kept thinking, Good God, Michael Harrison!

"What do you want to be?" I said. My voice sounded lame, like making-conversation time.

"A rock star, naturally," he said and laughed. "Hey, don't look so surprised. Haven't you noticed my charisma?" He was really laughing, head back, flash of perfect white teeth. "Everybody wants to be Mick Jagger, right?"

"I saw you in *Pirates of Penzance* at school; you were good," I said.

"Yeah, that turned out pretty good."

He started singing along with the song on the car radio. He was singing to himself more than to me, kind of grinning, thumping on the steering wheel. It was nice. I didn't have to make conversation—I could just sit

32

back and look at him. Perfect straight nose, the slightest suggestion of a dimple at the corner of his mouth. He even had a fairly good voice.

North Bay came too soon. That whole long bus trip was less than ten minutes by car.

"Where do you live?"

"Oh, I don't want to take you out of your way; you can just drop me off at the post office."

"Come on, where do you live?"

"You know where Varian's is?"

"Sure. That's a big three blocks off the Boulevard. I think I can make it."

"Thanks a lot. The bus would have taken forever."

"You mean you take the bus?"

"Yes."

"That's a downer. When's your first class?"

"Three-thirty."

"I have a private lesson with Pat at three-fifteen. If you don't mind getting there early, I'll drive you next week."

"That would be so great, thanks."

"Just remind me the day before, okay?"

"Okay."

I kind of bounced up the stairs to the apartment. There was the smell of meat frying, pork chops. Mom was already home.

"When I saw it raining like that," she said, "I didn't know what to do. I would have picked you up. I thought I'd drive over from work but—"

"It was fine, Mom, I—"

"But I didn't know when you'd be through or where you'd be. You must be soaked."

"No, I'm not, I—"

"I can't see why you have to go there anyway. That money could be spent for a lot more useful—"

33

"Oh, come on." Here we go again, I thought. "It is my money."

"Even so. You could use some new clothes, and I've got a stack of bills piled up. You're getting old enough to think about helping out."

Maybe if I didn't answer she'd stop.

"That place is overpriced to begin with, and if you add on the bus fare . . ."

"I didn't take the bus home. I got a ride."

"A ride? What do you mean, a ride? Who with?"

"One of the boys in my class."

"I don't want you taking any rides with—"

"Mom, it was all right. It was just a boy in my class."

"I don't want you hanging around with a bunch of musicians."

Sometimes I couldn't believe her. What musicians was she talking about? What was she so afraid of? Joseph Buccalati? Pat Calhoun?

"Mom," I said, "it was a boy who goes to my high school. He's no musician; he doesn't even play that well. . . ."

"From your high school?"

"Yes."

"Oh."

"He's not only from school, he's a junior and he has his own car, he's really cute and he lives in Ocean Point and . . ."

I could see Mom relaxing and getting interested. I listened to myself talking that way about Michael Harrison, and I knew I was doing it to make Mom feel better about the Guitar Institute.

"He sounds nice," she said.

"He's going to give me a ride next week, too, so . . ."

We had dinner and as long as the conversation was about Michael Harrison and things like that, Mom could be like a friend. As long as I kept guitar lessons out of it.

I was itching to tell someone about G.I. Well, I thought, I'd tell Jeff tomorrow.

Afterward, she set up the ironing board and worked on her good black skirt. She steamed it and pressed it, standing barefoot and shifting from foot to foot as if it were hurting to stand at all. She brushed the worn spots and steamed it again.

I took out my guitar and tried the fingering that Pat had shown me. *P-A-P-I-P-M.* It was pretty easy. I was glad that Pat used the Spanish initials for the fingers the way Joseph Buccalati had taught me. Pulgar, Anular, Pulgar, Indicio, Pulgar, Medio. I kept at it for a while.

"Don't you have some homework to do?"

"Not now."

"You should be doing more schoolwork."

"Later," I said. I should practice with a pick more, but I like fingerpicking better. *P-A-P-I-P-M, P-A-P-I-P-M.*

"I wish you'd stop wasting your time with that," she said.

I concentrated on the guitar and tried not to see her tired, strained face and her swollen bare feet.

"Good," Pat Calhoun had said. "Very nice."

"You can really play that thing," Michael Harrison had said.

P-A-P-I-P-M, P-A-P-I-P-M.

4

I called the American Federation of Musicians as soon as I came home from school. I was put on hold for a while and then a woman's voice told me I wanted Local 802. She transferred my call and then I was put on hold again. My hand ached from holding the receiver, and I started thinking that my call had fallen through a crack somewhere. Waiting. Our telephone is attached to the wall in the kitchen, and I stretched the cord as far as it would go, trying to reach the refrigerator. I really wanted something to eat, but I couldn't quite make it and I was afraid to let go of the receiver. I was beginning to wonder if Big Ray Bronson existed at all. Waiting. I thought of hanging up and starting all over again.

"Hello." A man's voice. "Is this the call for Ray Bronson?"

"Yes. Yes, it is."

"I can give you his service number. 555-5000."

"555-5000. Thank you."

"Okay."

Big Ray Bronson. I was going to be able to reach the huge black man with the beard after all. I don't know what made me hesitate before I dialed.

There was a crisp voice at the other end. "Five thousand."

"Hello," I said, "I'm trying to reach Ray Bronson." My voice sounded childish to me and the end of the sentence went up like a question.

"This is his service. Could I have your name and number, please."

"Linda Garcia. 705-8252. Oh, that's in North Bay; the area code is 516."

"Just a minute, please. . . . Mr. Bronson is on the road. He's due back in about four weeks. Could Mrs. Bronson help you? She calls in every few days."

Funny, I had never imagined a Mrs. Bronson. "No," I said, "I just wanted to speak to Mr. Bronson. Could you ask him to call me when he gets back?"

"All right. Is there any other message?"

"No, just ask him to call me, please, before six o'clock. Thank you."

I didn't realize until I hung up that I had been holding my breath.

Four weeks! More waiting. Waiting for Big Ray Bronson, waiting for Jeff's cousin at Beth Israel. I had to do something; I couldn't just sit around the apartment that afternoon. Aunt Katherine didn't get uptight if I asked questions; maybe I'd go over and ask some more.

My Aunt Katherine's house smelled of wet diapers and tuna fish, and it took a little getting used to. I babysat a lot for her that year while she took classes at Adelphi, and it took about ten minutes of being in the house before I stopped smelling it. I guess Katherine and her husband and the kids weren't even aware of it. The place was a mess, but I guess three kids in six years is a lot. Katherine was always busy with the dishes or she had the baby hanging on to her leg or something, but it didn't seem to faze her.

She did seem very surprised, though, when I told her about my father.

"Your father's dead?" She looked up from the button she was sewing on Meg's overalls and rested her hands in her lap. "I was on the phone with your mother yesterday, and she never said a word to me."

"She never does," I said. "She won't talk about him at all."

"She must have her reasons," Katherine said, and she went back to the button.

"I'd really like to know what they are. I mean, he was my father and I don't know anything about him at all."

Meg was making humming noises as she crawled and pushed a bright red car along the edge of the living-room carpet. The floor was littered with bits of colored construction paper, a Slinky®, and a large Big Bird®. I could hear Jimmy outside in the backyard with some other kids, counting off for a game, "One . . . two . . . three . . . four . . ."

"I thought you could tell me about him," I said.

"Linda, you keep asking, and I wish there was something I could tell you. I honestly don't know what to say. I was only sixteen when your mother got married, and it happened so fast. I just saw him a few times. She went on tour with him and then I was away at school, so I hardly knew him."

"Mom must have talked to you."

"No, not really."

"I'd think she'd talk to you more than to anybody," I said. I talked to Katherine a lot. She seemed a million years younger than Mom, more like an older sister than an aunt.

"Jeanne and I weren't very close in those days."

"You were so close in age and everything. If I had a sister, we'd be best friends."

38

"It doesn't always work out that way. We didn't get to be friends until much later."

"Why, Katherine? Was she terrible to you or something?"

"Oh no, Linda, it was all my fault. I had some growing up to do first. I was too jealous of her."

"Jealous of Mom?"

"Yes."

"Oh, you're not like that."

"Well, yes I was," she said. "See, when I was just starting high school, being Jeanne Quinn's kid sister was my cross to bear. It was awful for me."

"Why?"

"I was kind of awkward and super self-conscious; my nose was too bumpy and I wore braces and all that. And then there was Jeanne. I wish you could have seen how beautiful she was then. She had a kind of glow about her, all blond and fresh and shimmering. All I heard about was Jeanne Quinn. I wasn't 'Katherine'; I was 'Jeanne Quinn's kid sister.' She was a cheerleader, and there was this group of boys that made a thing of always sitting in her section at the football games, just to watch her. Can you believe it? Her own fan club. You know how mean kids can be sometimes. Guys would see me in the hall and say 'Hey, fish-face, send your sister over!' Ha, ha. That passed for wit at North Bay."

"It's still like that."

"There was one year, on Valentine's Day, the mailbox was jammed with cards for Jeanne, and her boyfriend that year gave her this big satin heart filled with candy. Isn't it funny, I remember it after all these years and Jeanne can't remember it at all. I can see that red-and-white-striped ribbon as if it were this morning. Anyway, there wasn't a thing for me, not one card."

"There should have been. I think you're so nice-looking." I wasn't just saying that, either. She looked so lively and healthy, and I couldn't see where Mom was any better looking.

"You're sweet, hon; yes, I'm a late bloomer." She laughed. "You know how your grandmother puts labels on things? Well, I was the smart one and Jeanne was the pretty one. Grandma had such big dreams for her. She was always saying Jeanne was a double for Lana Turner."

I must have looked blank.

"A big movie star in the forties. Did you know that your mother was Miss Teenage Nassau County?"

"Mom never told me that."

"No, I guess she wouldn't. Grandma entered her in a lot of stuff like that. Anyway, I was jealous as hell, so Jeanne and I were worlds apart. I never gave her a chance. It wasn't until years later that Jeanne told me she had always wished she were 'the smart one.' She used to wonder why I didn't like her. Being unhappy made me mean, you know? Jeanne passed by one day and some smart-aleck friend of mine sneered and said, 'Hey, Jeanne, say something to us in cheerleader.' Her face went bright red and what I did was laugh. So you can see why we couldn't be close then. When I got that scholarship, when I went away to college, I did fit in and that made all the difference. There really is life after high school."

"Mom got married right after high school, didn't she?"

"Yes. Jeanne was going with Harold Cummins in her senior year. . . ."

"Harold Cummins from the hardware store?" That seemed incredible. All I could think of was a large man behind a counter of light bulbs and hooks. All the times Mom and I had gone into Cummins's, I had never noticed anything special between them; they just said "hello" to each other.

"I thought you knew about that, Linda."

"No."

"Harold was North Bay's football hero that year. Football hero and golden girl, the perfect couple. It was near the end of senior year, and they went into New York with a bunch of other kids to celebrate something. I think it was after the Yearbook Dance. One of the places they went was the club where Silk Garcia was playing. I've heard he was a super showman and that audiences would hang on to his every move. I know Jeanne was dazzled. Well, obviously he noticed her. He was due to go on the road with a band, and she went with him and they got married in Chicago. She even missed graduation; they mailed her diploma to Grandma."

"She went off with him, just like that?"

"Just like that. It was the last thing you would have expected of Jeanne. She and Grandma were so close, with all the beauty contests and Grandma making her party dresses and the two of them chattering about boys and movie stars. She had always been Grandma's good girl. Well, Grandma was terribly hurt."

"What was he like?"

"Silk Garcia? I only saw him a few times. They were traveling a lot at the beginning, and I was away at school. I'm sorry, there's not much to tell you."

"Did she love him?"

"Yes, of course. She had to have very strong feelings to go off with him like that. When she left, she was radiant, eyes shining. She said she had never felt so alive before."

"I look like him, don't I?"

"Yes, you do."

"My eyes?"

"Yes, very much your eyes."

"Well, what was he like, really?"

"I don't think he was much older than Jeanne, but he seemed so much more . . . well, worldly, I guess, than the boys we were used to. He had a kind of . . . energy that you could almost feel. Even when he was just sitting still, his foot was tapping or his fingers, something was sizzling. When he was in the room, you were aware of him."

"Did you like him?"

"I sympathized with him. He tried so hard to charm everyone. Almost all the times I saw him, Grandma and Grandpa were there, too. Your grandfather was still alive then. You know how Grandma can be, asking a lot of questions and looking disapproving. I think he was uncomfortable and performing for them."

"Mommy, Mommy!" Meg had a loose wheel in her extended hand. "It broke!"

"Let me see, sweetie," Katherine said, and she started fiddling with the wheel. "See, you can push it right back in here."

"What did you mean, performing?"

"It was just a feeling I had, Lin. He talked about his people being from Catalonia in Spain. I've told you that before."

"A town outside of Barcelona."

"Right. I'm sorry, hon, I still can't remember which town in Catalonia he said."

"You were talking about him performing."

"There was a story he told us, for example. When he was a little kid growing up in New York, he'd hang out with the neighborhood Puerto Rican kids and talk Spanish their way, but when he was home, he had to remember to talk perfect Castilian or he was in bad trouble. His grandfather gave him a beating once with his gnarled old cane from the old country for leaving out the Castilian *th*. Do you know about that, *th* instead of *s?*"

42

"Castilian is what they teach in school. His grandfather. That's my great-grandfather!"

"He made it a funny story. He told it in a very charming way, doing different voices like an actor. He could make you picture this dignified, aristocratic gentleman, ramrod stiff with a large black moustache. I'm not sure it was all true."

"What wasn't true? Why?" I felt hurt.

"I don't mean it that way, that's unfair. As he talked, it seemed as if he were standing back and watching the effect he was having on you. Like a performer. He was trying to entertain and impress your grandparents. I sympathized with him because he couldn't reach them. I was just a kid; he didn't pay much attention to me."

"What about him and Mom?"

"They were living in the city where you were born."

I knew that much and I waited for her to continue, but she didn't."

"What happened between him and Mom?"

"I don't know. I was away when she came back to North Bay. Things just didn't work out between them."

"Aunt Katherine, I can think of dozens of marriages that didn't work out, but kids still get to see their fathers. I'm not even allowed to ask a question about him. Mom won't talk at all, and that's pretty weird. And he should have been able to come and see me all these years, because he was my father and I had a right to see him."

"Jeanne has a right to have her feelings respected."

I was surprised by the edge in Katherine's tone and she must have noticed, because her voice softened.

"Linda, I do understand how you feel. I honestly don't know what happened, but I think there was a lot of pain for your mother. When she came back here, her special glow was gone; she looked completely worn out, and if there's something she doesn't want to talk about, well, that's her business. You owe her that much consideration."

The voices of the kids playing outside reached a high pitch. Then Jimmy's voice, "Mommy, Mommy, they're cheating!"

Katherine put her sewing down with a resigned smile. "Here comes Mommy to the rescue." She rose. "You never really know, Lin. Who'd have thought that *Jeanne* would end up on her own and supporting herself? And in that store, waiting on women who remember her from high school!"

Another voice from outside. "I am not cheating!"

"You are!"

"Am not!"

"Are!"

"Not!"

Katherine turned and looked at me, hesitating, her hand on the knob of the back door.

"Silk Garcia is dead now. Leave it at that. Let it go."

5

I saw Michael Harrison from across the cafeteria every day, but he didn't see me. I would munch away at a sandwich and listen to Jeffrey, but out of the corner of my eye I watched the action at his table. There were lots of comings and goings, people stopping for a moment to say something, chairs crowded together, Michael laughing, his arm around someone. I wondered if I would have the nerve to remind him about giving me a ride to the Guitar Institute. The distance between our tables was too vast.

One day I passed him in the hall after Social Studies, and he looked right at me. He was walking with a redhead, Bubbles Something-Or-Other, and he grinned and waved. I waved back and that was all, but I had a really strange feeling in the pit of my stomach, kind of tingly and excited. I spent the rest of the day hoping to get another glimpse of him, but I didn't see him again until Tuesday.

When I met Jeffrey at lunch on Tuesday, he was almost squeaking with excitement.

"Hey, Lin, hurry up, sit down, I've got to tell you what happened!" He was bright-eyed and gleaming.

45

"Hi, Jeff."

"Lin, you know those charts I made, with color groupings and genetic possibilities?"

It took me a moment to realize that he was talking about the parakeets.

"Well, I showed them to Dr. Franklin, because he's getting into that kind of thing in class now, and he said my concepts were very sophisticated and . . ."

Jeff looked so happy, almost childlike, and I was glad for him, whatever it was.

". . . so he said I should enter the All-County Science Search, and he's going to recommend me! He said if the parakeets turned out the way I predicted that would be a bonus, my chances would be excellent, but even if they didn't, my charts were still interesting enough to make a good project."

"Oh, Jeff, that sounds great!"

"We talked for a while and he said a report explaining my theories would be fine, but to beef it up with some more thorough research. Look at this book list. I'm going to have to check out some of the libraries in New York. He's giving me a letter of introduction for the Columbia University library, so I guess I'll start there."

"What happens if you win?"

"Nothing, really. The most important thing is the prestige, I guess. The best part of this for me is the process, having Dr. Franklin for an advisor and having those library facilities open to me. There's some kind of prize money, a gift certificate for some minor amount, but that's not the point of this anyway. . . . Linny, just take a look at this. Dr. Franklin had some ideas. . . ." He was unrolling a long sheet of paper on the table. "See, it all depends on the baby parakeets. . . ."

I saw his shadow on the table before I heard his voice, low, amused. "What depends on the baby parakeets?"

Michael was standing next to my chair. He was smil-

46

ing at me, a special kind of smile as if we shared a secret.

"Oh, hi," I said.

"Sorry to interrupt you guys," he said. He flashed a smile at Jeffrey, then back at me. "I'm getting desperate for help, Linda. I was trying to figure out the stuff for tonight and I can't remember what Pat said." He handed his music notebook to me. "Where did I go wrong?"

Michael's arrangement was very messed up, so I started to make corrections and explain. Jeffrey was watching me silently and rolling up his sheet of paper.

"Oh," I said, "Jeffrey Breslow, Michael Harrison."

Michael nodded at Jeffrey, and I suddenly saw him through Michael's eyes. He looked about ten years old, scrawny, big ears, a nondescript shirt with the collar half-turned the wrong way. I bent over the page of music.

"Don't use a diminished seventh here," I said. I wrote in a few notes. "Okay, I think you can figure out the bass line from this." I gave him the notebook.

"Thanks, that's beautiful," he said. He started to walk away and then half-turned back. "Wait, do you need a ride today?"

"Well, yes."

"Can you be at the front steps at ten of?"

"Oh, sure."

"Okay, see you later."

I watched him threading his way back to his own table, waving here and there. His shoulders were muscular under the camel sweater.

"I'm desperate for your help, Linda baby," Jeff said.

"He didn't say 'Linda, baby.' "

"Oh wow, Michael Harrison talked to you! I never thought you'd join the Michael Harrison fan club."

"Oh, come on, cut it out, Jeff. He's nice."

"I didn't think you even knew him."

"I don't, really. He's in my class at G.I."

"Yay, lucky you. Can I be you and do Michael Harrison's homework?"

"It's a complicated arrangement, and he just had a little trouble with it, that's all." I was getting really annoyed.

"Wait a second, Lin, I was just kidding. If you say he's nice, fine, he's nice."

"He is," I said.

"Today we have"—and he was reaching into the brown paper bag—"we have . . . ta-dum . . . Smithfield ham and Swiss cheese on rye! Two chocolate brownies! An apple! A napkin!"

I took half the sandwich and thought, he is really the best friend I could ever have.

"You were telling me about your theory. . . ."

"Well, what I did was work out a theory of how a mutation might occur and how it could create a red parakeet. Then I made these charts showing my three generations of breeding and based on that, I make predictions on future generations. Okay so far? Now it gets complicated. If a mutation . . ."

"I'm listening," I said. And I did, all through the lunch period, barely glancing at the other table in the center.

I met Michael at the front steps at three that afternoon. The winter sun picked up the golden glints in his hair and again, there was that special warm smile, his eyes looking deep into mine, sharing a secret with me.

Three girls from Spanish class passed us and they shot a puzzled look at me, at him, back at me. I hoped someone else I knew would come along. Being seen with Michael Harrison was something to savor, even though it was only for a ride to G.I.

"My guitar is home," I said. "It'll take me just a second to run upstairs and get it."

"No problem."

He was driving slowly out of the parking lot. There were blocks in the circular driveway to keep people from speeding. There were kids walking, and lots of cars, so he was doing no more than ten miles an hour.

He asked what teachers I had and what I was taking. He had Morrison the Monotone for Geometry last year, and he had hated it, too.

"Don't do what I did," he said. "I slept all through that class, now don't you do that."

"It's so boring."

"Yeah, but I wound up with a C minus; you don't want to do that. You've got to at least try to stay awake."

It was that kind of conversation, about teachers and subjects we liked and didn't like. All very impersonal. That's why it seemed like such a non sequitur when he turned to me at a red light on Shoreview Road.

"Your eyes are unbelievable." He laughed and shook his head. "I can't believe that color."

I felt self-conscious with him again. "Just gray."

"No way. They're cat's eyes. I'll bet they glow in the dark, too." He looked straight at me, considering something. "The year of the cat."

I wondered what he meant.

Later on, in Arranging, I played my arrangement really well, I was the best in the class, and I felt him watching me.

Was it possible? I thought. Could Michael Harrison possibly like me?

School days dragged on by. It was a rainy February, and dreary, and I just waited for Tuesdays at G.I. I loved all of it: Pat Calhoun nodding and saying, "Right! You've got it, Linda!" and fitting in with the other kids and really being a part of things there. And Michael Harrison. Come on, Tuesday!

49

I dreamed through most of my high school classes. Sometimes I did finger exercises, trying to move each finger as far as I could without moving any of the others. That's hard with the fourth and fifth, and it's supposed to improve coordination for the guitar. . . .

"Miss Garcia, take the next question, please."

"Oh . . . uh . . . sorry, I've lost my place. . . ."

Sometimes I read the writing on the desks. I wondered why G. R. hated R. E. and loved K. M. And it was good to know that "The Stones are #1."

I did pay attention in Spanish, though. It was the one subject I really did want to take. I'm not sure of what I had expected. I suppose I thought I'd have a natural affinity for the language, but it was as foreign to me as to anyone else in the class.

Years ago, when I was still in junior high, a boy named Billy took me to the Spring Dance and tried to make out in the dark area of the hall near the stairs. When I pushed him away, he was kind of mad. "I thought all you Latin girls were supposed to be so hot-blooded." Latin girls? Me?

I knew all about the Quinns. They've been in North Bay since way back, the original clamdiggers. And before that, they came from Ireland and Scotland. Grandma even knew the names of the towns on both sides of the family. I didn't feel like a Quinn, though. I didn't feel like a Garcia, either. Whatever a Garcia was supposed to feel like.

I thought about the things Aunt Katherine had said. Silk Garcia's people were from a town near Barcelona, in Catalonia, Spain. I could almost see that aristocratic old grandfather, upset if Silk dropped the Castilian *th*. I spent a lot of time studying the map of Spain on the wall in the classroom. I found Barcelona in the upper-right-hand corner. I didn't know anything about Spain beyond what Miss Rosado had taught us and I stared back at the network of red-and-black lines. Maybe I even had relatives in one of those minuscule dots!

I was at my locker after my last class, and Michael passed by.

"Hi, Cat-Eyes," he said.

"Hi," I said.

He took a couple of steps down the hall, then changed his mind, turned around and came back. "I'll walk you home, okay?"

"Okay."

We went down the main steps and through the parking lot.

"Wait a second, I want to put these in the car."

He had an armful of books and papers. He tossed his things in and slammed the door.

"Are you just going to leave your car here?" I asked.

"I'll get it later. Hey, it's a great day. I feel like walking."

After all the cold weather, the warmth of a beginning-of-March thaw felt like spring. You could feel the sun, and there was a nice wet-earth smell.

I had never been with Michael except for G.I. and driving back and forth in the car. It seemed different to be walking with him. I was very aware of how tall he was and of the loose, easy way his body moved. I didn't have anything to say, but Michael was so at ease, so in control of everything. He talked when he felt like talking, and when he was quiet, it was a very relaxed kind of quiet. I wished I could be that sure of myself.

We followed the curve of Lloyd Hill Road. I had a prickly feeling, as though I were waiting for something to happen. We crossed the Boulevard and started down Main Street. We were walking close together, arms brushing, not saying much. I wondered why he was walking with me and whether he had planned to go into town anyway.

We stopped at the window of Ace Records. A Led Zeppelin album, Billy Joel, the Talking Heads. A poster of Mick Jagger in skintight satin pants. A Bo Derek poster. Michael started singing snatches of the song that was played on WPLJ so much that month.

> *If you like my style*
> *And wanna try me for a while*
> *Come on, come on, come come closer . . .*

He was kind of laughing, kind of mocking the lyrics. We passed Gino's, and he asked if I wanted to stop for pizza. I said, "No, thanks." I was still too full from lunch, Mrs. Breslow's salami and rye, but I thought it was really nice of him to ask.

> *You know what you wanna do*
> *And babe, I'm red hot for you*
> *Come on, come on, come come closer . . .*

We stopped at Varian's window and looked for a while. He said something funny about the ceramic bulldog and we laughed. There was a look in his eyes, though, and it had nothing to do with the bulldog. When we came to the building doorway, I thought he would continue on down Main Street. I hadn't expected him to come all the way up the stairs with me. At my door, I fumbled with my keys, really awkward and nervous. I glanced up at him and away; I couldn't meet his eyes. My mailbox key, the door key, the key to my gym locker . . . I could barely get the door open.

"Anyone at home?" he asked.

"No," I said, "my mother's at work."

He followed me in. I unzipped my jacket, and it sounded incredibly loud.

He kissed me then, his body pressing mine against the wall near the kitchen door. His lips were so soft and so warm. I hadn't expected his lips to be so warm. His tongue flashed across my teeth. Michael Harrison kissing me, I thought. I couldn't believe this was happening. We kissed and kissed for a long time. His hand was moving around under my jacket. Part of me was lost in shivery feelings and part of me was thinking, I'm acting like some kind of groupie. Why am I doing this? I could have pushed his hand away, but I didn't. Then we were on the couch, kissing some more, pasted together. For just a moment I thought, he's so sure of himself, he doesn't even have to lead up to anything. His mouth tasted of peppermint gum.

When he left, he gave me a slow good-natured smile and said, "See you tomorrow."

The next day, being with Michael Harrison like that seemed unreal. I looked at him in the halls when I changed classes, but I didn't see him around anywhere until lunch. When I walked into the cafeteria, I saw the back of his head, sandy hair with just a few tufts of gold where it met the tan neck. The memory of how it felt to have my fingers in his hair suddenly hit me, and I could feel the color rise in my face. He was in the middle of the crowd, and I wondered if I should go over to say hello. He turned around and saw me.

"Hey, Linda, over here!"

He was waving me over, smiling that beautiful smile.

"Move over, everybody, make room for Linda."

There were two tables and a lot of people jammed together. They adjusted and shifted, and there was space for me next to him. I knew some of them. Jan Matthews was a sophomore, too, and in my English class. I knew

Beverly Cramer from junior high; she was beautiful even then, with alabaster skin and a perfect, tiny nose. Ron Gilroy, the president of the student council. Bubbles, the redhead I used to see Michael with all the time.

Bubbles was talking. "So then Sonny said, 'If you guys are all going to Beverly's party . . .' "

Michael put his arm around me and whispered in my ear about Beverly's party and who Sonny was, so that when Bubbles finished the story, I could laugh along with everyone else. And then they were talking about Friday night and skating at Iceland.

Beverly said, "I'll need a ride."

"I can get you on the way over from Linda's," Michael said, and then to me, "I'll pick you up early, about eight, so we won't have to stand in line. . . ." I nodded and tried not to notice that he hadn't asked me.

Jan said something to me about the English homework and seemed very nice and friendly.

I couldn't believe it could be so easy. Michael Harrison said I was in and so I was in, as simple as that.

It wasn't until I had almost finished lunch that I happened to glance into the corner near the beverage counter and saw Jeff sitting there all alone with an empty chair and an overstuffed lunch bag.

6

Sometimes Michael and I went up to my apartment during free periods or lunch. No one was
supposed to leave school during the day, but lots of kids
went to Gino's Pizza and hardly anyone ever got caught.

There was a special feeling to the apartment during
the day, when no one was supposed to be home and the
rest of the world was at school or working or something. There was a special quiet, punctuated by an oc-
casional gurgling of pipes in the wall and faraway traffic
noises from the street. Inside, it was so quiet, just
Michael and me, our ragged breathing, the creak of the
couch, and the buzz from the refrigerator.

I memorized him with my fingertips. His beautiful,
beautiful mouth. The tiny triangular scar on his chin,
white against the golden tan. The smoothness of his
muscles and my skin melting into his. All the cliché
song lyrics became profound. Mick Jagger's "Wild
horses couldn't drag me away . . ." went straight to
me. I must love him, I thought. And still—something
kept holding me back.

"Come on, Linda."

"No."

"Come on, come on, you're old enough and I'll be careful. . . ."

"No. No, not yet."

My body was fused to his, and my breath came in crazy gasps. So this was what it was all about. "Wild, wild horses couldn't drag me away. . . ."

It was an effort to surface into the real world. It was a colossal effort to check the time. I had two free periods back to back, but they wouldn't last forever.

"We have to get back to school," I said.

"What for?"

I never cut school. I didn't really think about it. It was just something I never did, and I was surprised that Michael was so casual about it.

"Let's go, I don't want to be late."

"Oh, lady, you can't go now. . . ."

"I have Geometry."

"Linda, come on, let's stay awhile."

"You have a class, too." I was struggling up from the couch.

"I don't care. Let's stay."

"No, listen, I really have to get back."

"Come on, baby, this is more fun than Geometry."

I felt that special ache, and it was in Michael's eyes, too. "Do you want to come over later, this afternoon, after school?"

"No, I have that SAT review, damn it!"

"That doesn't make sense." I was up and out of reach.

"What doesn't?"

"How come cutting school doesn't bother you, but you have to go to those SAT things?" I was brushing my hair into place.

"You don't know my father. He's paying for it and if I skip one, I'm dead!"

"Wouldn't going to all your classes do you more good?" I didn't think private tutoring for the Scholastic

56

Aptitude Test would be more important than showing up for regular classes at school.

"I don't care about the SATs; it's my father's trip, not mine. It's easier not to argue with him. You'll meet him one of these days, and you'll see what I mean."

Hearing Michael say that pleased me. It was like— *Ping*, a quick mental note: I'm going to last for a while. It seemed as though Michael was always taking the lead and I was just tagging along at the edge of the group. It was only at the Guitar Institute that we were equals. I still didn't know why he had chosen me and I didn't feel as if I had any hold on him at all and I hoped I would last.

"He's pushing for me to break 1200 in the SATs. He went to Dartmouth and he wants me to apply there."

"What do *you* want?"

"Sex 'n drugs 'n rock 'n roll."

"No, really."

"I don't have the slightest idea. For my dad, everything is winners and losers. Getting me into the right college is winning, right? And he likes to come out on top. I'm not sure I want to play the game."

"What does he do?"

"He's a lawyer. He's very good at it, too, and I really admire him. I just don't like his style."

"Are you interested in law and all that?"

"You're kidding. Can you picture me some high-powered lawyer up to my ears in that shit? I couldn't care less," he said with a big smile.

Lots of kids said they didn't care about one thing or another, but they were really in there, straining. Even Michael's crowd. The acted so nonchalant, but you could feel them trying for the right image. One day LaCoste was in and designer jeans were out, and then Docksiders were out and Timberlands were in, and it changed so fast, I couldn't begin to catch up with all the

57

signals. I thought Michael truly, honestly didn't care and that's why he was so easy to be with. I wasn't even embarrassed about our apartment. Mom had terrific taste and used tons of white paint and plants and made great-looking drapes out of sheets, but things got worn and chipped, and there was never enough money to replace them. Even though Mom tried so hard, it did look shabby and after all, Michael was from Ocean Point. But from the very first time, I could tell Michael didn't even see it.

"So if you want me," he was saying, "it has to be now because I won't be around before Friday."

"I'll try to survive."

"What difference does one class make? *One* class?" He was sprawled full-length on the couch and stretching lazily.

I was watching a shaft of sunlight catch his wrist-watch and turn the hair on his arm to gold. When the telephone rang, it made me jump.

"If that's my mother," I said, "she'll want to know what I'm doing home."

"Your mother wouldn't be calling an empty apartment, would she?"

It rang again.

"Do you think it's the school or something?" I said.

"No."

I made it to the kitchen halfway through the next ring.

"Hello."

"Hello. This is Ray Bronson."

"Oh, yes!"

Everything had been feverishly Michael Harrison. I went to school and thought: Michael Harrison. I practiced guitar and thought: Michael Harrison. Silk Garcia and Ray Bronson had receded far into the background.

"Linda? I had a message to call you."

"Yes, thanks so much for calling back."

I was very conscious of Michael on the couch in the living room with just a paper-thin wall between us.

"What can I do for you?" The deep, rumbling voice.

"I know you were my father's friend." I tried to keep my voice down without actually whispering. "I'd like to talk to you."

"Oh?"

"About my father."

A beat. Then, "Does your mother know you called me?"

"No."

"That's the way it is, huh?"

"I don't want to impose on you." I tried to remember the warmth I had felt from him. "I need to know more about my father, and I'd really like to talk to you." Please, Michael, don't hear.

"Yeah, I can understand that."

"I don't know where you are, I mean, where you live or anything."

"I'm in Manhattan."

"Could I . . . well, I could get into the city . . . could I come to see you?"

"Sure. Anytime."

"Would tomorrow be all right?"

"Fine. How's one o'clock? You can come up for breakfast."

"I'll be there."

"It's 403 West Seventy-fourth Street. Apartment 6D."

"I'll be coming from Penn Station."

"Right. Take the IRT Seventh Avenue express up to Seventy-second. You'll see the Beacon Theatre. It's a couple of blocks over. Okay?"

"I'll find it. Thanks, I really appreciate it."

"It's cool. See you tomorrow."

I stayed in the kitchen for a moment. No turning back now. I hoped Michael hadn't heard my end of the conversation. I didn't want to explain.

When I came back into the living room, all he said was, "Come here, I saved a warm spot for you."

He hadn't been listening; I was relieved. I couldn't talk to him about my father and that whole thing. It was Jeff Breslow that I wanted to talk to right now.

"Michael, I really want to get back to school."

"What's the matter?"

"Nothing. I just want to go."

We had a few minutes before the start of the next period, so Michael and I were hanging around in the hall with some of the other kids. Beverly was there and Ron and Bubbles. Everyone was kidding around and laughing. Ron was in the middle of a story when I saw Jeff Breslow turning the corner at the far end of the hall.

Jeff didn't really know any of them, so when I was with the group we'd usually just say "hi" from distance. I kept thinking that sometime I'd tell Michael about how special Jeff was and then maybe they would get to know each other and be friends, but somehow the opportunity never arose.

This time, Jeff must have been very excited because he came rushing right over to me as soon as he saw me, rushing right over without thinking.

"Linny! Guess what! The greatest thing happened! The feathers came through, and one of the babies is almost pink! Lavender, really, but with a lot of pink!"

Somebody giggled. Jeff looked startled, as if he had just realized that he was right in the middle of everybody.

"Yippee! A pink baby!" Another giggle and somebody laughing.

"That's great, Jeff," I mumbled. My face was getting

60

warm, and I couldn't look at him. "I'm really glad."

I could feel his eyes on me. The giggler was still at it.

After a moment, he backed away. "Well . . . good-bye, Linda."

"So long." My voice sounded funny.

I watched him go down the hall, walking fast.

"Hey, Linda, who's your friend?" That was Ron.

I wanted to go after Jeff, run to catch up with him, but I couldn't just run away from Michael and every-body. And what could I say to him? Anyway, the bell rang and Jeff was going in the opposite direction from my next class and, well, I'd talk to him later. I hurried to Geometry. I especially didn't want to be late because I knew I'd be cutting the whole day tomorrow to see Big Ray Bronson.

7

The bright sunlight emphasized the pockmarks on the buildings, the faded awnings, the dinginess of the street. 403 West Seventy-fourth Street. This was it. The hall had a worn maroon carpet and smelled faintly of mildew. There was a wizened elevator operator and an old-fashioned elevator with an iron filigree door. It creaked slowly upward. Apartment 6D. There was a strange feeling in my stomach. Probably because I hadn't eaten lunch. If I were in school, I would have had lunch an hour ago. I should be in Social Studies now. But instead I was about to burst into a complete stranger's home to ask a lot of questions. No, I reminded myself, not a stranger. Big Ray Bronson had been my father's friend. I took a deep breath and rang the doorbell.

The door opened wide and Ray Bronson's immense body filled the frame. He was wearing a fuzzy, violet sweater, vivid against his massive dark brown neck.

"Come in, come on in. You found it all right?"

"Yes," I said, "it was easy."

"Well, come on in. Anita, this is Linda, Silk Garcia's kid."

I knew there was a Mrs. Bronson, but I hadn't expected to see her today. She wore glasses and a nurse's uniform.

"Hello, Mrs. Bronson," I said.

She acknowledged me, unsmiling.

I was startled by the room. It was covered by thick pearl-gray carpeting. Really covered: floor, all four walls, ceiling. Otherwise, it was kind of empty, just a few large pieces of furniture, much too modern for the building.

"What did I tell you, Anita, it's Silk all over again," he said.

"It's uncanny," she said. It was hard to read her face, grave and deadpan. I tried to catch her eye and couldn't. I suddenly thought, she disliked my father; she dislikes me.

"I'm just having breakfast," he said. Breakfast at 1:00 P.M.? He steered me toward a huge, low white table. There were cups and coffee things, strawberry jam, a plate of toast and Danish, an enormous glass canister of pastel afterdinner mints.

"Sit down, Linda, and have some coffee-and."

I sat down and so did he, on large gray-carpeted pillows. Mrs. Bronson didn't join us.

"What'll you have?" he said.

"Just coffee, thanks." I didn't usually drink coffee, but I thought not taking anything would seem rude. I didn't think I could swallow anything solid.

He poured for me and slathered his toast with jam.

"Didn't mean to scare you the other day." Most of his face was hidden by the full beard. There were deep lines around his eyes. "The resemblance . . . well, I'd say I overreacted."

"Oh no, you didn't." I felt stiff. "Thank you very much for seeing me today, Mr. Bronson."

"Ray, okay? Relax, Linda, everything's mellow." He was smiling. "Now what can I do for you?"

"That other day, when you were talking to my mother, it seemed like you knew my father very well."

"Yeah, I did."

"I wondered if . . . You see, my mother won't talk about him at all, so I hardly know anything about him."

Did I imagine it or was there a quick look between Mr. and Mrs. Bronson?

"Excuse me," she said, "I'll have to be leaving for work. Very nice to meet you." Very polite, very aloof.

"Very nice to meet you, too, Mrs. Bronson," I said. I felt more comfortable when she was gone.

"So you want to know about Silk. I can understand your feeling. Well, I played with him on and off for years, you know, one group or another."

"Did you know his family? Could you tell me about them?"

"No, when I knew him, he wasn't living home anymore."

"Did he ever tell you anything, like about his grandfather from Spain, or anything like that?" I had a clear vision of the aristocratic, proud old gentleman with the gnarled cane from Aunt Katherine's story. My great-grandfather.

"Grandfather from Spain? No, honey, he came from the Dominican Republic. I never heard anything about a grandfather."

"When he lived with his family, wasn't there his grandfather . . .?"

"No, there was no family, just Silk and his uncle. Rosario, I think his name was. They lived up on 110th. There was some kind of problem with Silk's mother so they sent him up from the Dominican Republic to live with his uncle. Where'd you get a grandfather from Spain?"

"I don't know," I said, "I guess someone told me."

"Yeah, well. Stories would get around about Silk.

64

For the right chick, he'd weave an ornate tale." He laughed. "Sometimes he was a Cherokee Indian."

"Oh. Could you tell me about his uncle, then?"

"I never met him. I know it was the uncle who showed him how to play guitar. Flamenco, that kind of thing. Silk said that was the only good thing the man ever did. And that's about all he said. I'm sorry, I don't know anything about his family."

"I thought you would."

"No, I met him later, when he was on his own."

I sipped at the coffee. "Then, could you tell me about my father later on, I mean, when you knew him?"

"I'll try. How do you describe a man, where do you start?" He reached for a candy mint.

"Please, tell me anything at all," I said. "Tell me about the first time you met him."

"The first time I met him. . . ." He crunched the mint and took another. "No, I'll you about the first time I *heard* him. I didn't *meet* him until much later."

He smiled at me and leaned back, remembering.

"The first time I heard him . . . I was with Lucky Harris's old group then."

"*The* Lucky Harris?"

"Yeah, right, that was a cookin' group." He smiled broadly. "Well, we were doing the Apollo, and after the last show, I'd go on down to Baby's on 124th Street— that was Baby Esther's. It's burned down now. That's a lot of years gone by. . . ."

He was deep in a memory, and I waited for him to continue.

"Well, in those days, Baby's was the place, you know, anybody who was in town would stop in after their gig and most nights the jamming went on until six in the morning. Now I'm talking about Lester Young stopping in and Dizzy and Charlie Mingus, the baddest of the bad, and there was this kid, Howard McCrory,

65

just a local kid who was pretty good on the drums. He was somebody's half-brother, I forget whose. Well, the first time I saw him, Silk had been tagging along with McCrory for a while. I don't think he was any older than you, a skinny Latino kid, maybe fourteen, maybe fifteen. He was the only white face in the room, so yeah, I guess I noticed him for that. But not just for that. He was so hungry to sit in. Now let me explain something. You can't go ahead and *ask* to sit in with cats like these, you got to be *invited*. He'd be sitting off by himself, doing all this flashy fingerwork on his guitar, no sound, not plugged in or anything, but he was looking out of the corner of his eye for someone to notice. He'd stay all night, listening and taking everything in with those weird glow-in-the-dark eyes, itching to get on and getting a big ignore. Until finally one time Jimmy Jefferson stopped in. You know who Jimmy Jefferson was? He came out of Louisiana, real old-timer, played a mean guitar and got a lot of respect. Well, that night, the old man was going strong and there was this kid, doing his finger pyrotechnics, staring straight at him.

"Jimmy ignored him for a while, but you could see he was getting bugged. Finally it got to him too much.

" 'All right, let's see what the little mother can do,' Jimmy said.

"So Silk came up, real cocky with this kind of strut he had. Jimmy laid on a couple of chords and I got into it with the horn, real slow and easy, and at first the kid had it, played some nice lines. A lot of the guys picked up their ears, you know? But then Jimmy started going into fast changes and the kid couldn't make it. He couldn't keep up, no way. Man, he started to sweat and fall apart. Jimmy got disgusted with the whole thing, just stopped playing. And everybody else slid to a stop. There was a silence. I mean, a heavy silence. No expression on the kid's face, real cool. His eyes went blank.

He got up and unplugged himself and all you could hear was these taps he had on his shoes, like all the Puerto Rican kids wore at that time. Esther was behind the bar, a big fat woman, and she started to laugh. He walked out of the place, no one talking, not a sound, just the click-click-click of the taps and the echo of Esther's laugh."

Bronson stopped. The silence he had been describing slipped into the room, and I couldn't say a word to break it. He reached for the candy mints. Not one at a time, the way you would normally eat them. He gulped down a handful.

"Four years later, everybody was talking about the great new guitarist with Johnny Lonigan's group, so I went down to catch him. Right, it was Silk Garcia. He was playing like nobody else. Man, he made the hairs on the back of your neck stand up. Then over the years we played together with one group or another, and we were pretty tight. So I found out what happened.

"That night at Baby Esther's, he knew some stuff from his Uncle Rosario and what he'd picked up here and there, but not all that much. See, Silk sometimes had this puffed-up idea of himself, very unreal sometimes, that's just the way he was. So he thought he was a hotshot until he got ranked at Baby's. Now this is what happened. He couldn't keep up; he didn't know keys, and he was too proud or too much the loner to ask for help like anyone else would do. No, he tried to figure it out all by himself and he reinvented music theory. Right, *re*invented. Can you dig it? Can you picture this kid picking away at his guitar in some little room someplace, discovering the circle of fifths, for instance? He'd never heard of Bach; he had no way of knowing that those eighteenth-century cats had figured it out already. He was too dumb to know that most jazz was played in five, maybe six keys, so he went and taught himself all twenty-four. I mean backward and forward. He was making sure he'd never get ranked that way again, and he wound up playing like no one else, going in and out of keys you never even thought of, using flamenco, blues, jazz, all mixed together. He was a brilliant guy, a true genius.

"There's always a line of progression. Silk took from Django Reinhardt and Charlie Christian, and all the guys that came up later and took from Silk Garcia. He was right up there with the giants, and I'm not just talking guitarists, okay? My trumpet style changed from listening to him. I don't know how technical you want to get—like he'd play a bar in nine-quarter time broken up into three bars of two and one of three. Like this." He was beating it out for me with his knife against the table. "No one was playing anything like he did."

I had always known he was good; I knew that from "Blues for Linda Ann"—but "brilliant," "genius," "up there with the giants"! This was more than I had expected. It more than made up for my lost fantasy of Barcelona: my aristocratic great-grandfather, my vision of dark-eyed women with mantillas like on the red-and-black Maja soap wrapper. No, this heritage was better. Silk Garcia, Giant of Jazz. And I was Silk Garcia's kid!

Ray Bronson must have seen it all over my face, because he smiled and nodded, like he was telling me to go ahead, be proud.

"I think I'll have a Danish, after all," I said.

"These are cinnamon-raisin. They're good." He slid the plate toward me.

I shifted on the pillow, took a pastry and leaned back a little. I could feel my whole body relaxing. "This is a nice room," I said.

"The padded cell? It's not too bad."

"Padded cell?"

"Soundproofing." His laugh was a deep rumble. "It's

68

either that or eviction. Anita would love to have ordinary walls sometime."

"Did Silk ever come here?"

"Yeah, often. He holed up here sometimes, a couple days, maybe a week, like when he needed to get his stuff together."

I looked around the room and imagined him sitting there, on the tan cushiony thing near the window, or here, on one of these pillows. I thought of him being in this room touching this cold marble table that I was touching, walking across this floor. I could feel his presence all around me, settling over my shoulders, warming me.

"What I don't understand, though," I said, "is that I couldn't find anything about him. There's nothing printed, nothing in books, no one's ever heard of him."

"Musicians know about Silk Garcia. What you're asking is why he wasn't famous."

"Yes."

"That's a fair question. There's no simple answer to that one."

He was pouring another cup of coffee.

"Silk's improvisations were always inventive and smooth. Silk, smooth as. That flow came when he was feeling loose, playing in a club, dim lighting, smoke-filled room, a drink on the piano and some woman with moist lips grooving on it. Now picture a recording session. It's called the 'record industry.' *Industry*. Session set for ten in the morning, Silk's been up all night, sandpaper in his eyes. Some exec in a suit and tie giving orders, a voice from the control booth talking about sound levels. Bright lights and cues. Silk wasn't adaptable and, no, he wasn't at his best on records."

"Did he make a lot of records? I only know about one."

"He cut some with Johnny Lonigan. They'd be under

69

Lonigan's name. And then it was Silk's bad luck that just when he was coming up, the dark ages began."

"Dark ages?"

"Silk was just about twenty and starting to make a name for himself, working at Domino's. But then there was a whole period when one jazz club after another closed down. Birdland and Basin Street and Stuyvesant Casino and finally even the Embers. They all went. There's a disco where Domino's used to be. Talk about your dark ages. The sixties were a wasteland for jazz. Well, Silk was married by then and you were born and he was looking for some bread. I played a stage show with him, part of a big band, a revival of the vaudeville-show-with-the-movie kind of thing. I can't remember which theater, I think it was the Capitol on Broadway. We ran four weeks. Four weeks of the same jokes, same music, an hour and a half each show. Vocal number, dance team, comedian, 'A funny thing happened to me on the way to the . . . ,' drum roll, magic act, impressionist, curtain. We'd doze between shows and listen to the movie going on. Same actors, same lines, same inflections, frozen on film and then the on-stage buzzer and we went on with the same arrangements, same notes, da-da-da-dum, frozen into the same routine. Silk, going on and off like a sleepwalker. 'Man, I feel the moss growing up my leg.' The big finish was the impressionist. He'd get to his Elvis Presley routine, and that was Silk's cue to play a couple of chords. Another show, applause, movie goes on and a bunch of the guys go down to the bar on the corner to fortify themselves for the next one. That's the way it was, grubbing for any kind of gig, and maybe it was hardest on Silk. Silk Garcia, playing the same two chords, staring out at the audience, everything going downhill."

He was quiet, remembering, not looking at me.

"Yeah, well," he said finally. He looked infinitely sad. "Michelangelo painting Burma Shave signs."

What about Mom, I thought. Had she run out on him when everything started going downhill? I couldn't find a way to ask that one.

Instead, I said, "Did you know my mother well?"

"Jeannie? Oh, sure, while she and Silk were together. You should have seen her. She was like a flower that had just unfurled. When you were born, they had that apartment in the Village, just off MacDougal, and they were good together. Silk, you know, was a nighttime guy and suddenly, there he was, walking the baby carriage around Washington Square Park. A sight to see, Silk tipping his hat to the other mothers and asking about some baby's colic." He laughter rumbled. "Man, he enjoyed playing that role! Silk Garcia, going straight. And Jeannie, with that one-hundred-watt smile. I always liked her."

"My mother never talked about him. I never saw him in all those years, and it never made any sense to me at all. What really happened?"

He crunched another mint. He took too long to answer, and I could see that he was choosing his words very carefully.

"I don't know," he said. "I've told you about all I can. Look, honey, if you want to know about your father, listen to his music. It's all there. Whatever else he was, the music was the heart of him."

Ray Bronson gave me a snapshot of my father before I left. I felt self-conscious about examining it in front of him. I thought I would wait until I got on the train.

When I left the building, it was still sunny, but the wind had started blowing. My hair whipped around into my face, and bits of debris were zigzagging down the sidewalk. I saw her coming toward me, walking close to the building side of the street. She was a very old lady, pale, thin, slightly bent over. She was carrying two grocery bags, one in each arm. They weren't large, but you could see that she was straining. The wind was pulling at her coat and then a gust caught her little navy felt hat and carried it across the sidewalk. It was all a split second: the dismay and helplessness on her face, the people rushing by, and my sidestepping to retrieve the hat. I gave it to her and took one of the grocery bags. She was flustered and trying to hold her coat closed with her free hand. Her skin looked dry and stretched across the fragile bones. She was going only half a block, to a torn striped awning that said HOTEL BEACON. She thanked me with a slight accent, said she could manage now and disappeared into the revolving door. That was all, but as I went down the subway stairs, I kept seeing her face in that moment of helplessness. She would have lost only a hat, so I don't know why it made me feel so bad. Something about being vulnerable on a busy city street.

Then, in the subway, I noticed the girl sitting across from me. She was no more than twenty, with coffee-colored skin and reddish hair in the remains of an elaborate hairdo. She was wearing a green knit dress, no coat or jacket, and she was fast asleep, breathing heavily through her mouth, her head bobbing up once in a while and then falling heavily against her shoulder. She had pretty, feminine features: a small, soft-looking nose and smooth skin except for a discolored patch on her forehead. The dress was stylish but covered with stains. Stains of different colors that looked as if they had gotten into the green knit at different long-ago times. I didn't smell any liquor, so it wasn't that, but you could tell there was something terribly wrong.

I was glad to get out of the subway with its top decibel roar and its Day-Glo graffiti. Was this Silk Garcia's New York? I had a bad feeling that didn't lift until I was on the Long Island Railroad heading toward North Bay.

On the train, I studied the snapshot Ray Bronson had given me before I'd left. Silk Garcia, Ray Bronson and another black man, all holding instruments. Bronson looked much younger. It must have been taken long ago.

Silk Garcia. He looked like a kid in his twenties. Longish straight hair and high cheekbones. He was staring straight at the camera, not smiling, and his eyes did look a lot like mine. I studied the eyes for a long time and tried to read the expression in them, but there was none. No expression at all. They seemed opaque. Maybe it was because of the way the sun was hitting his face. He was wearing a white long-sleeved shirt, open at the collar. Silk Garcia. I could feel his image imprinting itself in my mind. I would forever see my father as twenty-odd years old, staring into a camera.

"A giant. . . . No one was playing anything like he did." My father didn't have to take a back seat to anyone, and I was so glad I knew that now. I did look like him. I did take after him. I could feel it!

It wasn't until later, when I was gazing out of the dirty train windows at that swampy place near Douglaston, that I started wondering about the other things. The strained way Mrs. Bronson had acted. Some of the things Bronson had said. "He holed up here sometimes. . . . Silk Garcia, going straight. . . . Whatever else he was, the music was the heart of him. . . ."

Ray Bronson had been so warm to me that I almost hadn't noticed how carefully he was choosing his words.

Sooner or later, I'd have to piece together the rest of Silk Garcia. Sooner or later, I'd have to meet someone who didn't know me as his daughter. I'd have to find out about the "whatever else he was. . . ."

8

If it hadn't been for Michael, Mom would never have let me go to Geronimo's.

He came over for the evening, and she liked him right away. He gave her that warm, intimate smile that I thought was just for me at first. By this time, I had seen him use it often; on salesgirls, teachers, waitresses, and now, on Mom.

"I'll be honest with you, Mrs. Garcia," he said, "this place is a dive. It's just that our teacher at G.I.—you know, Pat Calhoun—well, he's playing there on Saturday and a whole crowd of kids is going over to hear him. It'll really be all right."

"I don't know," Mom was saying. "First of all, they'd never let a fifteen-year-old in."

"They check double IDs, but we'll have some by Saturday; it's all set," Michael said.

"I just don't like the whole idea."

"Mrs. Garcia, I won't have any more than one beer, I promise you." Full-caliber smile. "These kids we're going with, they're all completely straight. And if I see anything that looks like trouble, I'll take Linda and drive her right home."

74

He was radiating sincerity and Ocean Point class. Mom finally said I could go. Before he left, he kidded with her for a while, telling her how cool she was for an adult and all that. She started kidding back and for just a moment, she looked a little flushed and very young.

"He's nice," she said later. "I like him a lot."

"So do I, Mom."

"I'll bet he's one of the best-looking boys around."

"All the girls like him," I said. I could sense Mom respecting me for Michael. I was finally doing the right thing.

"The first boy you really go out with, well, you'll always remember him. I'm glad it's Michael," she said. She was filing her nails with an emery board and she frowned, concentrating on one spot. "Maybe I'm wrong to let you go to Geronimo's. There's not going to be a lot of drinking, is there?"

"No, of course not. We're going there to hear Pat, that's the only reason."

"Where is this place, exactly?"

"Seaford."

"Seeing you with Michael brings back a whole flood of memories." She looked soft and wide-eyed. "Like getting fake proof and going out and . . . High school was so much fun. . . ."

I was surprised by her admitting to fake IDs. She was usually so extra careful to be superproper, as if someone were observing her, grading her. She had stopped filing and was looking off into space.

"What are you thinking about, Mom?"

"Oh, nothing, really. Thinking about you growing up and the boys I went out with in high school and how I felt when I was your age. . . . It was such a nice time. . . ."

She seemed so warm and open, I thought I could chance it. Maybe we could really talk.

"And after high school, Mom? When you first met my father . . .?"

That was a mistake. The mask slipped back on and suddenly there was a TV program she had to watch. A door slamming shut. I hated it when she went deadpan like that. It was like coming home from school to an empty apartment when I was just a little kid; all the silence and getting my own snack and eating all by myself. She was giving me that same hollow feeling. But I wasn't a little kid anymore.

I watched her. Expressionless. The zombie. I couldn't tell if she was really watching the program or not. There were lines under her eyes and deep ones from her nose to her mouth. Mom looked okay for somebody's mother, but beautiful? No way. Aunt Katherine had said "beautiful . . . a glow about her . . . all those beauty contests." And Ray Bronson had used the word "beautiful," too. Funny, that was just about the only thing anyone had said about her. There must have been more to her than that.

Saturday night, going to Geronimo's. I had the double IDs safely tucked in my jeans pocket—someone's driver's license and library card. Irene, the girl I had met on my first day at G.I., had made all the arrangements. A whole bunch of kids were going and it would be fun. Actually, I had been invited first and I was bringing Michael along. I wondered if he had noticed that. The group at school always invited Michael first.

We were whizzing down the Boulevard in Michael's yellow Ford. Yellow is the color of happiness, I thought. With wheels, everything was within reach and anything was possible. We were heading south. The hills and trees of the North Shore gave way to long, flat stretches of road, lined with used-car lots, houseware stores, fast-food joints, a neon jumble of "Appliance

Center" and "Discounts." Geronimo's was squeezed between a paint supply store and a garden center. In front, there was a brightly colored plastic "wooden" Indian.

"God, that's so awful, it's perfect," Michael said.

We walked into a solid wall of smoke and noise. It was a small, dark place with rough wooden benches and tables, jammed with college-age kids. College age, but definitely greaser types. The smell of pot was so strong, I wondered if I'd get high just by breathing. There was a long, crowded bar and the band on a slightly raised platform at one end. Drums, bass, keyboards, two guitars.

Some of the G.I. people had arrived before us and were holding a table. There were nine of us all together. I focused on Pat at the bandstand. I thought he was terrific, and I really looked forward to hearing him. But it was rough. The G.I. table was the only one that was listening and quiet. The people at other tables were yelling at each other in order to be heard over the amplifiers.

"Yo, three Molsons over here!"

A snatch of nice lead from Pat and then the keyboards. . . .

"Hey, you wanna pizza with anchovies?"

Drums and Pat and . . .

"Mac's drunk as a skunk! Ha, ha, ha, ha!"

Rolled-up T-shirts and tattoos and sideburns. It was wild and I felt bad for Pat, but when he came over to say "hello," he was relaxed and laughing.

"Anybody got a beer for me?" he said and Tommy slid one over.

"Linda, Mike, glad you made it," he said. "This place is the pits, huh?"

"It's awful," I said. "How can you stand it?"

I must have looked really upset, because Pat came

77

over to my end of the table and leaned over with his arm around me.

"It's okay, Linda."

"It's awful, you're too good for—"

"Linda, listen, all right? You came in at the wrong time. We do one of our own numbers once in a while, just to keep sane, and that's when they tune out. Bedlam." He shook his head and laughed. "When we play cover music, it's fine. They only want to hear something where they know the words."

"Pat, how can you put up with—"

"Wait, you'll see. It's not a bad audience if you know how to work them."

He was right. For the next number, they turned up the amps and did an Allman Brothers thing, and the crowd was banging out the rhythm on the tables, rowdy but enthusiastic.

The waiter came to our table with a couple of large pizzas and started taking drink orders.

"Beer all around?"

"Michael," I said, "I really hate beer. Could I have a glass of wine, please?"

Michael raised his eyebrows. "You hate beer?"

That's what I had been drinking at parties with Michael's friends all along, one beer, just not to stick out, and I really hate the taste of it. Here, surrounded by G.I. people, it felt like time to start having what I liked.

"How come you never said anything before?"

"I don't know. Anyway, I'm saying it now."

He shrugged. "You want some Chianti?"

"Sure, that sounds great."

They served the wine in a carafe. It was good. I poured another glass.

Pat was doing lead guitar and back-up vocal. They were playing a lot of Southern Rock and I knew that wasn't what he liked, but I could see that this crowd did. Pat and the band were working them up to a high pitch. The sound and the beat were crashing all around me.

Pat stopped by our table again and took a mouthful of beer, swished it around his mouth before he swallowed.

"Jesus, I'm getting hoarse," he said. "Does anyone want to sit in for me on 'Satisfaction'? You know the lead, Larry."

"Hell no, not me," from Larry.

"How about you, Linda?" Pat said. "Here's your chance."

"Oh, no," I said. "I couldn't. . . ."

"Why not? It'd be a good experience for you. Just plunge in, baby."

"No, I . . ." and then I thought, of course I could, I knew it backward and forward, I always liked the Rolling Stones, why not? I stood up and drained the last bit of wine from my glass and said, "Okay, Pat."

He walked me up to the band area, his arm around me. "You've used my guitar before; you know the lead; just do any damn thing you please. It's all yours." A quick introduction and a nod from the rest of the band.

I thought I would quietly slip in, but the G.I. table started to cheer me. I knew they were trying to help. They were feeling good and they were on my side, but they attracted the attention of other tables, and people started looking around to see what was happening. The place quieted down, and everyone's attention was on me, waiting.

"Who's the chick?" a voice boomed out.

Now there was a real air of expectancy in the place and I thought, oh, my God! My heart was pounding so hard, I thought it might show through my sweater. The adrenaline reaction, Biology 1, fight or run.

The drummer got it started and with the first bars there was a roar of recognition from the crowd. Oh

God, Pat had given me a present! "Satisfaction" was a classic and anyone short of a cross-eyed monkey should be able to get this crowd with that anthem!

I wished I had something of Silk Garcia's to bring me luck. My heart was pounding. A lucky penny, a magic pendant, anything . . . but I do, I thought, I do, I do, I do, I have the genes!

The drummer's thump–thump–thump–THUMP–THUMP! went right through my body.

> I can't get no
> Sat-is-fac-tion
> I can't get no . . .

The beat was getting to the crowd and then the strangest thing happened. I felt waves of energy coming right back at me, physically, palpable waves of energy hitting me.

> 'Cause I try
> And I try . . .

It was getting higher and higher. I was bending notes and putting a scream into that vocal. The crowd screamed back at me and we were passing it back and forth; I could feel it in my chest, in my gut, thousands of little explosions.

> And I try
> And I try . . .

I was burning hot and moving with the beat and the crowd was moving with me and we were all one.

> Hey, hey, hey
> That's what I say . . .

My hair was swinging in wild arcs behind me.

> *I can't get no*
> *I can't get no . . .*

I was sweating. I could feel sweat on my face and the crowd was screaming the words out with me and those electric shocks were ricocheting back and forth and I was shattering into a million pieces.

> *Sat-is-fac-tion*
> *SAT-IS-FAC-TION . . .*

I ended with the guitar raised high in the air, head back, panting, wet.

> *SAT-IS-FAC-TION!!*

Pat took the mike. "That was Linda Ann Garcia! Linda Ann Garcia! All right, Linda!" He hugged me and I hugged back.

I went back to the table with the sound of stamping and whistles and "All right!" all around me. Pat's group had the amps way up now and I had more wine and Michael kept his arm around me. I had dived right in and the water was warm.

Much later, Michael and I were driving back along the Boulevard.

"Should I take you home or do you want to park someplace or what?" he said.

"I'm too wide awake." I was still bouncing inside. "I don't want to go home yet."

"What about your mother? I don't want to get her down on me."

"She's probably asleep. She worked all day today, and anyway, she likes you so much. You can't do any wrong."

"Okay, great, we'll park down by the—"

"Michael, listen, can we just walk around for a while?"

"Just walk around?"

"Please. I feel all keyed up."

"Yeah, all right, if that's what you want."

We left the car at the end of Main Street and walked over to the Town Dock. There wasn't a soul around except for the night watchman in his booth. We walked over to the far end, right over the water. The sailboats were rocking gently in their moorings. The bay was black, with just the reflected lights of the Sea Haven restaurant in the distance. The only sound was the gentle slaps of the waves against the dock.

It was so peaceful, but I couldn't stand still. I looked out into the water and snapped my fingers and sang softly. "I can't get no . . . I can't get no . . ."

Michael laughed. "That was dynamite tonight."

"It felt so good," I said.

"Yeah, I know. That's the way I felt in *Pirates of Penzance*. Remember that scene when I came in . . ."

I didn't remember. The school play was long ago, when Michael was a distant idol. God, everything had changed so much! He went on about the scene and I wasn't listening.

". . . and that was a real high," he finished.

"That's the way I felt tonight," I said, "a real high."

"I never saw you like that. I didn't know you had it in you."

"How do you mean?"

"You got up there and you took over. You came on so strong. You ran over the rest of the band like a bulldozer."

"Did I really do that? Did I do the wrong thing?"

"Hell, no, you were great." He was smiling at me. "What got you going like that? Was it the wine or what?"

"No, I'm sure it wasn't the wine."

"Talk about star quality. I'll tell you a story. My dad does a lot of theatrical law, contracts, things like that. One of his clients is this soap opera star. She's been the star of the show for years. She *is* the show. Anyway, I went to a party with my folks one time and she was there. There were a lot of people and a big buffet. Among other things, there was a mound of chopped liver. No big deal, but she happened to like chopped liver a lot. So what do you think she did?"

"What?"

"She spit into the chopped liver."

"She what?"

"She spit into the chopped liver so nobody else would have any, and it was all hers. I mean, she announced it like it was a big joke, but she really did spit into it and no one else took any, right? Later, going home, my sister said how obnoxious that was, like she couldn't believe it. Well, my dad said that was star quality. That's ego and grabbing the whole pie for yourself. That's how she runs that show and gets herself nominated for Emmys and the whole bit."

"She sounds awful."

"I guess she is. She's funny and bright, though."

"Why are you telling me this? Was I spitting in the chopped liver tonight?"

"No, nothing like that." He laughed. "I don't know what the moral of that was. But you really did take over, and I didn't know you had that kind of drive. You were fantastic."

"They were my people!" My arms were stretched out, embracing the air. I whirled myself around.

"Did you catch that next table? They looked like Hell's Angels. Jesus, one of them had a safety pin stuck through his ear."

"Hey, hey, hey . . ." I sang softly. I was moving with it. "That's what I say . . ."

"Look out, you'll wind up in the water."

"I don't care."

"It's too cold," he said. "When it warms up, we'll go skinny-dipping."

"Off the Town Dock?"

"No, I'll find a more private place."

His hands were on my hips, and he drew me toward him. When we kissed, it was very warm and friendly, but I was too drained to feel sexy. Michael could tell, but it didn't matter.

He grinned at me. "I think you peaked at Geronimo's tonight."

"I guess so." I grinned back. I had never liked him more.

We walked back to the car, our arms tight around each other. Strange, after all those weeks of making out and everything, it suddenly felt as if we were friends for the first time. I wasn't sure of where it had happened. Somehow I had started believing in myself and stopped being in awe of him, and it made everything different. I'd have to figure it out later.

We sat very close to each other all the way home.

"Irene was talking to me before we left," I said. "She has a friend at North Bay High; he plays bass with Thin Ice. Do you know them?"

"Yeah, I think so. One of them was in my French class."

"They won the Battle of the Bands thing at school last year. Anyway, she says they want to dump their lead guitar. He's nothing but trouble, and Irene says she'll talk to them about me. They get almost all the dances around town. I'd have to get an electric guitar of my own, though, and they're so expensive, so I don't know. . . ." I was rattling on at top speed, unable to stop.

"She says their guitarist is a doper or something. He doesn't make rehearsals, and they can't stand him, anyway. It would be so great if . . ."

We stopped for a red light and kissed until someone honked behind us.

"I wasn't taking anything from Pat tonight," I said. "He gave me that as a present. I wasn't spitting in his chopped liver, was I?"

Then, finally, I wound down. I was suddenly so tired. My throat hurt and my eyelids felt as if they were drooping. I could have dropped off to sleep immediately, right there in the car.

"I want to tell you something else," I said. "My father was Silk Garcia. He was a jazz guitarist, and he was a genius. He reinvented music theory."

Michael didn't react. He had no way of knowing how good it felt to share that with him.

"Listen," Michael said, "hold off a while before you do anything about Thin Ice, okay?"

"Why?"

"I have an idea I want to work out. Just check with me first, okay?"

"Okay," I mumbled. I was dozing.

Going upstairs, we held hands. When we said goodnight, his lips just brushed my cheek. Nothing ever felt more right.

9

The day started crisp and sunny, and by lunch-time it was close to seventy degrees. The first really warm April day. Michael and I sniffed the air; you could feel summer coming on.

"You know what," Michael said, "let's go to the beach after school."

We stopped at Michael's house on the way, to pick up a blanket and stuff. It was a letdown. I had expected something grander—tennis courts, a swimming pool, miles of lawn. A lot of Ocean Point houses were like that. Michael's house was nice, but just a large ranch with a lot of bushes and trees and a jam-up of cars in the driveway. He parked at the road and his sister came out as we went up the walk.

She nodded my way, smiled automatically and went on talking to someone in the house.

"Hurry up, Anne! Get the wagon out of the way, will you? I'm late!"

Inside, there was wood-paneling, large windows with sunlight streaming through, slate floors and pale leather furniture. We came to Michael's room. It looked like the rest of the house, woody and beige with streamlined furniture, except for the fact that it was totally littered. Sweaters rolled in balls on his bed, socks on the floor, papers strewn all over the desk and spilling out of a wastepaper basket.

"Your sister looks a lot like you," I said.

"Only not as good-looking." He was rummaging in the closet. "I know there's a blanket in here somewhere."

I sat on his bed and straightened out and folded a blue cashmere sweater. It wasn't an imitation; it was the real thing; the label even said MADE IN SCOTLAND, and it was unbelievably wrinkled from having been dumped on the bed. His carelessness with good things kept amazing me. Mom had overprogrammed me to make things last, and I would have liked to let go, the way Michael did.

"You know your room's a mess."

"So what?"

I was looking at the tangled underwear on the floor.

"So now I know you wear Jockey shorts."

"I've given you every chance to discover that before." He pulled out a blanket and then tossed a jacket over to me. "Take this, it'll be cold on the beach."

It was a jeans jacket with a furry lining that I had seen Michael wear to school a million times.

"It can't be that cold," I said.

"You'll see, it's on the point. You'll feel the wind."

The beach was right on the point. The road turned into a dirt path that was blocked by a chain. We left the car and walked a little way through beach grass.

"I've lived in North Bay all my life and I never knew this was here."

"Hardly anyone uses it, even in the summer. The regular Ocean Point beach is down a way. They don't even bother to rake this part. Nice, huh?"

"Nice."

I used to go to Harbor Beach a lot, the public beach for North Bay, and it was all right, but you could see factories and the Long Island Lighting Company building across the harbor. That kind of ruined the effect. Here, there was nothing but beach and water, the bay on one side, the harbor on the other. Sand, beach grass, a tide line of rocks and broken shells, some large jagged gray rocks jutting out over the water. The only sign of civilization was the blanket that Michael had put down.

"You're right about the wind," I said and I put on his jacket. It smelled like him: peppermint gum and unidentified ingredients, the Michael-smell. I loved wearing it.

We climbed up on one of the large rocks. There was a flat plateau on top. It was hard climbing, and I scraped my hand before we finally got settled. Michael was sitting with his profile to me, looking out at the water.

"You look like the figurehead on a ship."

"I like it up here," he said. "I used to sail a lot."

"Used to?"

"We still have a boat. At Hedman's Marina."

"Don't you use it?"

"I do sometimes. Not often."

The closed look on his face made me curious. "Why not often?"

"*Y* is a crooked letter."

"My Mom used to say that when I was little. It made me crazy."

"Your mom's a together lady," Michael said.

"Not necessarily. . . . Why don't you sail anymore?"

"No big deal," he said. "When I was a kid, I kind of took to it. This was when I was eleven or twelve. They had kids' races at the club, and it was fun until my dad got interested. One time, there was this junior race, you know, with other clubs on the bay, and I came in third for my division. I was feeling pretty proud of myself

88

and then I saw my dad storming around on the shore. 'Why the hell didn't you come in first?' This was in a Blue Jay. Well, the next week, he equipped that Blue Jay, the best that money could buy. With an edge like that, man, there was no way I could lose. I lost my taste for racing, that's all. I still sail once in a while, just cruising around. I'll take you out sometime."

"That's so sad."

"No, it's kind of funny, if you think about it. I played soccer, too. Can you picture him on the sidelines, yelling at a bunch of ten-year-olds 'Kill that son-of-a-bitch!' He's a maniac."

"Sometimes I think everyone's parents are maniacs, one way or another."

"Maybe so. There was a big blowup last night because I'm not going to those SAT review classes anymore."

"Oh, I forgot, you were supposed to go today!"

"Right. Well, I've had it. I'm not planning on taking the SATs, and I'm not going to college right from high school, either. I just want to feel free for a while."

"What are you going to do?"

"That's what I've been thinking about. Did you know Pamela Mallory?"

"No."

"She went to North Bay for a while. Well, she dropped out, and I hear she's with a punk rock group in the Bahamas and having a ball. Isn't that the greatest?"

"I guess so."

"I've been meaning to talk to you about this ever since that night at Geronimo's. We could make one hell of a good team. Now I know you're twice the musician I am . . ."

Three times, I thought, and I hated myself for having let that pop into my mind.

". . . but I could do back-up chords and we'd both sing, and I have all that old charisma. . . ." That lovable smile again. "With Thin Ice, all you'd be doing is some local dances, that's nothing."

"Well, where would we be doing all of this?"

"That's the good part. One of my dad's clients in Dan Stein. He may not be a household word like William Morris or MCA, but ask anyone at the Guitar Institute. He handles all the top acts. It's just about impossible even to get to see this guy, but my dad can set it up for us."

"Why would your dad . . . ?"

"He thinks I'm talking about a summer job, so he's all for the idea. Listen, Stein books talent for the Hamptons, too, and there's this place in Easthampton called Windows, it gets a big summer crowd."

"Windows. I've heard of it."

"They use kind of low-key acts. I'm talking about acoustic guitars and ballads, no hard rock. Anyway, my cousin has a house in Easthampton. We could stay there and we'd have a ball."

"Do you think we have a chance?"

"Why not? Stein owes my dad some favors. I'm thinking, if it works out for this summer, then we get more bookings and take a couple of years off. All play and no work. Can't you picture me surrounded by groupies?" He was smiling.

"We'd have to get a lot of material together and . . . Michael, are you really thinking of dropping out?"

"For a while, at least."

"The only kids I know who dropped out are working at the gas station and the five-and-ten."

"There's dropping out and there's dropping out," he said. "We don't have to decide anything now. See what happens."

I couldn't imagine anything bad ever happening to

Michael. He had so much confidence, and everything seemed within reach for him.

"Michael do you really mean it? Would this man see us?"

"May 14."

"What?"

"We have an appointment with him on May 14."

"You didn't even ask me first?"

"I knew you'd love it."

"My God, that's so close. We have to get some stuff together and work on it. . . . Make sure you don't say anything to my mother about this."

"We should think of a catchy name," Michael said. "The summer's going to be a blast!"

"Oh, God, Michael!"

We clambered off the rock and jumped around on the beach.

"Do you love it?"

"I love it!"

"Are we a team or what?"

"We're a team!"

"It'll be excellent!" he said.

"This is so good!"

It was too much at once. A chance at a real job and flashes of the way it would be: Michael all summer and practicing with him every afternoon, the big break and Easthampton and Michael, Michael!

"We're a great combination," he said.

"I know we are."

I was breathless, watching him come toward me. Then we were standing with his arms around me and he was licking my ear and my arms were around his neck and his hand was under my shirt and he was pressed hard against me and my knees were almost buckling. For the hundredth time, his hand reached into my jeans and for the hundredth time, I pushed it away, this time in slow motion.

"You've got me climbing the walls, Linda. Stop holding out."

The same scenario but this time, when I thought of my reasons—I wasn't sure enough of him, of myself, I was afraid, I was too temporary in his life—none of them applied anymore. Everything had changed.

"I love you," he whispered.

His hand was there.

"Are you sure no one ever comes here?" My voice was husky.

The sharp intake of his breath and the pain-pleasure expression on his face.

"No one ever comes here."

I was crossing a line, and I would never be the same again.

"It's all right, Linda," he said. His lips were on my neck, in my hair. "I'll use something."

"Oh Michael, I love you so much," I whispered.

He released me and went to get the blanket and I watched him and I felt the absence of his hand and I was trembling. He held a corner of the blanket, dragged it along the sand and led me toward the dunes. We passed beach plum and tall dry grass brushed against us.

There was a moment just before he touched me again. Time stopped. It was quiet, like the eye of a hurricane, and we looked at each other gravely and then the special warmth of his smile released something deep inside me. Then his hand was moving slowly and my body strained to his. Our breath became frantic. Tangled jeans. The line between his golden tan and the paler skin beneath. April sunlight and the faraway sound of waves.

When Michael dropped me off, I forgot to return his jacket. It was warm in the apartment, but I kept it on all evening. I was supposed to be feeling guilty, but I kept remembering the way he had looked at me just before. I could still feel his fingerprints on me. I inhaled the peppermint gum smell of the jacket and ran my hands along the roughness of the denim sleeves. I thought of being with him all summer long. I was supposed to be too young but—oh God, I loved him!

"Linda, do you have a chill?"

"No, Mom."

"Then why are you wearing that jacket? I hope you're not coming down with something. . . ."

"No, I'm fine."

I was trying to act normal, hoping she couldn't tell. Maybe someday I'd be sorry, but I couldn't worry about that now. I kept thinking about Michael on the beach, and it made my insides contract. So this was what it was all about. I wondered if this was the way it had been for my mother when she ran off with Silk Garcia.

10

At first, everything was so absolutely perfect. At school, we held hands all through lunch, looked into each other's eyes and smiled. We had all these private jokes now and memories and people we both knew at G.I. and May 14 to plan for. I used to feel left out when he and Bubbles talked about things that had happened long before me. No more.

We were going to practice every afternoon after school. That first afternoon we flew at each other as soon as we got into my apartment, and we couldn't stop touching. We never did get the guitars out of their cases.

"I've been waiting for this all day," he said afterward.

"Oh, Michael, me, too." All day at school, I had been feeling like half of something that was struggling to come together.

"It gets better and better," he said.

" 'Wild, wild horses couldn't drag me away . . .' That's what I keep thinking."

"Do you want to do 'Wild Horses'?" His skin, his hair, everything looked golden in the afternoon light.

"Yes, that's just how I feel. Nothing, nothing, nothing could keep me away from you now."

94

"We'll work on it tomorrow. . . ." he said.

The rest of the afternoon was a golden glow.

The next day I did get my guitar out, and I showed him some things that I had practiced. I wanted him to do some chords to back me up, but he ran his fingers down my arm and along my leg, and the guitars lay forgotten on the floor.

Later, I said, "May 14 isn't that far away. We have to get to work on this."

"Don't worry," he said, "we'll get to it."

We didn't that afternoon, but I practiced by myself, after dinner, far into the night. I should have been studying for the Spanish test, but . . .

One day, when we finally got our guitars out, he was supposed to do a left-hand hammer and pull-off. He had trouble with it, and I asked him to keep doing it. I could see him getting bored.

"Linda, it's good enough for now."

"No, it's not. Keep doing it."

"You're kidding. How long do you expect me to do this?"

"My God, Michael! When I was ten years old I spent a solid hour getting the hammer right! My fingers weren't strong enough, so I'd work on it for an hour at a time. I don't see why you can't."

"Jesus, this is supposed to be fun."

"This is supposed to be serious. Come on, Michael!"

And then he was next to me and his hands were everywhere and in the midst of the shivery feelings welling up—I was wondering if he was just trying to stall.

But there were good practices, too. One day everything went right. We sang "Wild Horses" with all the feeling in the world, and we had fun improvising on some other tunes.

"Hey, we sound great! We're good!"

We tried to think of a name for ourselves.

95

"What's wrong with Garcia and Harrison?" I said.

"Try Harrison and Garcia," he said. "No, that's too nothing. No one'll ever remember that."

"Simon and Garfunkel did okay," I said.

"Yeah, but think along the lines of Peaches and Herb, the Captain and Tenille, something catchy."

"The best name I ever heard for a local group is Long Island Expressway," I said.

"But it's taken. Anyway, it sounds like heavy metal. Thin Ice is pretty good. Too bad they had it first."

We were throwing names at each other.

"Jericho Turnpike!"

"Fast Lane?"

"Sunrise Highway. Sunrise?"

"Sunrise Service. Room Service!"

"Nassau Nudies for the X-rated crowd!"

"Fresh Puke for the punk rock freaks!"

"One group that never made it," he said, "because the name was so dumb: the Beatles. Hey, how about the Maggots?"

"Listen," I said, "let's get back to work. Come on, Michael."

"Yeah, all right," he said. "How about the Sloth and the Shrew?"

We went to a Grateful Dead concert at Nassau Coliseum. We were two carloads of kids. We parked at the far end of the lot and wound our way through to the entrance, past the ticket scalpers and the hawkers calling into the cool night air.

"Tickets! Who needs tickets?"

Calling softly into the cold night air, "Reefer. I got good reefer. Maui Waui. Purple Sens. Speed. Speed here. Good mesc. Ups, downs and all arounds."

We had great seats, right near the front. ("My father can always get these tickets," Michael said. "One of his clients . . .") There was noise and excitement mounting, and then the lights went down and the show was on. Amplifiers shrieking, Grateful Dead-heads in Indian gauze skirts dancing in the aisles, Frisbees and beach balls sailing overhead. And at the end, when the lights went out: everybody all around the Coliseum holding up matches and lighters, stamping and yelling until the Grateful Dead came back for the encore. I was caught up in it, too, loving it, and in love with Michael, sitting next to me, all over again. At the same time, I felt outside it, watching, thinking. I looked at the six men on the stage, and they were just guys. They must have been nowhere once, maybe playing in pick-up high school groups, maybe at places like Geronimo's. It could happen for anybody. I had told Pat at the Guitar Institute about Dan Stein, and he had said, "Hey, that's great! He's very important!" As the Grateful Dead and the cheers and stamping trailed off, I was thinking, it could happen for me, too.

"You need more style," Michael said.

We were looking into the large mirror over Mom's dresser. He was standing behind me and holding up my hair with both hands.

"How do you mean?" I said.

"Your hair."

"I thought you liked my hair."

"I love your hair, but it's too North Bay. I think you should have it cut."

"I don't know. . . ."

"We have to look special. We want to knock him dead."

"Why can't we just go in looking like ourselves?" I was staring at myself in the mirror. "I could have my hair trimmed."

"Where?"

"I always go to Louise's on Main Street. Why?"

"Louise's is nothing. I want you to have your hair really styled. I mean in New York. My mother and sisters go to Guy Heron. All the models go there."

"Have it cut *short*?" I was so used to my straight bangs and long straight hair. It had been like that almost as far back as I could remember.

"I'm not saying short. I don't know. Just go to him and let him do it."

"I can't do that. I can't afford someone like Guy Heron."

"Don't worry about it; I'll pay for it. My mother has a charge account. . . ."

"I can't do that. I'd really feel funny about it."

"Look at it this way. Think of it as expenses for the act."

"I don't think so."

"You can't go in looking like another teen-ager from the suburbs. Come on, Linda, we'll go to New York for the day and it'll be fun. Let's do it next Saturday."

Guy Heron's was just off Madison Avenue. The reception-room walls were covered with yellow paisley fabric that had bits of red and blue in it. The furniture was white and curved, with matching yellow paisley cushions. There was a large crystal vase on the front desk filled with fresh red and yellow tulips. It could have been somebody's beautiful living room. The only thing that gave it away was the smell of shampoo and hairspray.

A woman waiting near us wore an immaculate white suit and pink eye shadow. I felt intimidated. Michael looked completely at ease.

"Harrison, please." Michael had made the appointment in his name. "Down the hall to the right for your kimono."

The kimonos were the same yellow paisley. When I had mine on, a woman steered me into a little stall and someone else washed my hair. It was wrapped in a yellow towel, and I was sent to another room. There was a long line of chairs in front of a mirrored wall.

"Guy, I'm going to miss my plane if you don't take me next." The voice was soft and cajoling, not at all anxious.

Guy Heron was working on a woman next to me. He was a deeply tanned middle-aged man in a business suit and tie.

"Darling, be patient."

I felt strange. Everyone else seemed to know him well. They were talking about things I didn't understand and laughing. I looked at myself in the mirror. My clogs were scuffed. My hair was hanging down, wet, and I looked so simple compared to everyone else.

Then Michael wandered in and I felt better. Michael, coming through this whole roomful of women, was relaxed, in his element, enjoying the glances his way. I didn't think there was another boy in all of North Bay High who could have pulled it off.

"Hi, Mr. Heron!"

"Hello, Michael, it won't be long. . . ."

It was, though. We waited forever. Finally, it was my turn, and he ran his fingers through my hair.

"What's your name, dear?"

"Linda."

"Now, Linda, what do you have in mind?"

"I don't know." I felt panicked.

"Something very different and theatrical," Michael said. "She'll leave it up to you."

Guy Heron moved my hair around in his fingers and studied my face in the mirror. "I'd like to cut it very short and frame your eyes for a very striking look. How does that sound to you?"

He seemed serious and professional.

I took a deep breath. "Okay."

The scissors flashed, and he seemed to do everything with a speed and sureness that made me trust him, but I couldn't look. Chunks of hair were falling down and being brushed off my shoulder. I glanced in the mirror, and all the hair was off my neck. I felt light-headed. There were deft movements with a comb and a blow-dryer. My hair was really short all over, a jagged fringe around my face, and it didn't look like me.

"That's it, Linda." He held up a mirror and swiveled my chair around so I could see myself from all sides. He was smiling. "Do you like it?"

"That's fantastic," Michael said.

My eyes looked enormous, framed by spikes of hair. My cheekbones stood out in high relief. "Oh yes, I do," I said. I really did. I'd have to get used to it, though.

He flicked the hair on my forehead. "What I've done is followed the shape of your eyebrows to emphasize your eyes. . . . You look beautiful, dear." He was already combing someone else's hair. "Regards to your mother, Michael."

On the way out, I said, "Michael, what do you think? Is it too extreme?"

He hugged me. "You're a knockout!"

We walked along Madison Avenue, hand in hand, feeling good. There was a store window with the thinnest silk dresses, floating in incredible colors: pale, pale green, lightest lilac, with something sparkling, all against a background of silver. I couldn't stop looking. We passed a jewelry store, and there were diamonds and emeralds against black velvet. A model rushed past us, elegant, streamlined, clutching a huge portfolio, hailing a cab.

We turned the corner and wandered into Saks Fifth Avenue. I caught glimpses of myself in the mirrored columns; it was like coming upon a stranger. Was that me with those huge eyes and that jagged cap of dark hair? We browsed in the men's department and tried on some Stetsons, posing, looking at ourselves in the mirror. Michael was adjusting my hat, and I could see him enjoying my new look. I leaned against him. We really looked great together. Michael stopped to look at some Italian sweaters, and the salesgirl treated him with respect. He was dressed like any other kid, just jeans, but somehow she could tell there was money in his pocket. When he asked for service, it was with that smile, and she brought out stacks of sweaters. He wasn't buying, and for a moment I felt bad, thinking of Mom and somebody doing that to her. But he was enjoying himself so much, delighting in all the colors, and he couldn't know anything about really needing the commission.

We passed one of those sample makeup bars. We stopped and he held my face very gently and put silver eye shadow on my lids. I didn't care if the silver looked freaky or not. There was something so sweet about the way he was holding me. My lips brushed his, right there in the middle of Saks Fifth Avenue, and I knew I would remember this moment forever. On the way out, he sprayed me with Joy and I sprayed him with Aramis and we left, smelling very expensive.

Later we stopped at the huge atrium of the Citicorp Center, sat at one of those little wire tables and listened to chamber music for a while. The light was diffused and the violins sounded very sweet. We held hands on the tabletop, nibbled at chocolate-dipped fresh strawberries from the confectionery store and admired each other. I felt pampered and polished.

The kids at school and at G.I. liked my new look. So did Pat Calhoun.

"That's *some* haircut!"

"Thanks," I said. "Michael thought I needed more style."

There was amusement in the coal-fringed eyes. "Baby, you've got style to spare."

I examined his face and the crooked grin to see if he was teasing me. I didn't think he was. He made me feel special.

Mom liked my hair, too, and asked who had cut it. I told her it was a new guy at Louise's and felt guilty about lying. Anyway, Michael was right about my new image, and I wish we could have held on to the nice feeling we had that day in New York. But our practice sessions were making us more and more edgy. Michael kept bringing up irrelevant things.

"Maybe you should wear a dress," Michael said.

"No, I'll be nervous enough anyway, so I want to be sitting with the guitar balanced on my knee. I'm going to put my foot up someplace, a chair rung or something, so I'd better wear pants."

"All right. What pants?"

"I don't know." All I had was jeans.

"What if we both wear all white?" Michael said.

"Okay." I did have a pair of white Lees.

"If we spend the next couple of days getting very tan . . ."

"We'd better spend the next couple of days practicing."

"Do you know that you're getting pretty damn compulsive?"

"Do you know that it's pretty damn ridiculous to think a tan will make any difference?"

The afternoon practices weren't enough. I had started putting in a lot of time in the evenings, too. It was funny, the more I got into rock, the more I thought a good lead should be playing jazz. So I was playing jazz guitar, too, and then getting into the classics again. Carulli exercises to keep my fingers strong and Villa-Lobos Prelude no. 1 to make sure I could still do it. And a Travis pick once in a while, just for fun. I played anything, depending on how I felt. It was like eating potatoes or bananas or caviar, whichever way my appetite went. It was all nourishing. Sometimes my fingers hurt or my hand was stretched just too far or I couldn't sit still for another minute, but at the same time I could get outside my body and keep on going and feel enormous peace.

"How much more of that?" Mom said, irritated. "Don't you have any homework?"

"I did it all this afternoon."

Not true. I failed a Spanish test for the first time. My book report for English was going to be late. Geometry was dropping to a C. But May 14 was coming up, and I was going for broke.

11

May 14.

We were a half hour early. When we sat down on the receptionist-room couch, I left an air space between Michael and me. I didn't want shoulders grazing, elbows touching, nothing. I was dry-mouthed nervous, and I wanted to think my own thoughts, get myself ready. But Michael kept leaning into my space and talking. I guess he was nervous, too.

"See, we would have had time for coffee. We should have stopped at that place downstairs."

"I didn't want any," I said.

The room was small but expensive-looking. Carpeting, sleek receptionist.

"We're lucky we didn't get stuck in traffic," he said. "We made incredible time."

I am Silk Garcia's daughter, I thought.

"It's good to come early, though," he said.

I can handle this, I thought, I know I can.

"You want some gum?" He held the pack in front of my face.

"No." I always come through, I thought. No matter

how scared I am, when the time comes, I always do all right.

"Or a Life Saver?"

Except once, I thought, that time in fourth grade when I played for the class. I was going to do "Freight Train." I didn't know that nervousness would turn my fingers into lead. I wound up playing it like a dirge.

"Jesus, I hate waiting," he said.

The nervousness doesn't go into my fingers anymore, I thought. I can control it now.

"Getting that spot down the street, having that guy pull out just as we came by, that's a good omen. We could have circled around for an hour. . . ."

The talent show in junior high, "Silent Night" at the chorus Christmas concert, that wonderful night at Geronimo's—all those other times, I did fine. Anyway, I thought, this is for only one man, not an audience.

Michael was flipping through a magazine.

I am Silk Garcia's daughter, I thought.

"There's a Szechuan restaurant on Third Avenue that—"

"Please shut up, Michael," I said.

"Jeeze, you're great company."

He stepped over his guitar case and went to talk to the receptionist. I watched him give her Ingratiating Smile #3 and I watched her respond to him.

He sat down again and we waited some more. I watched the receptionist type, answer the telephone, type some more.

I've felt like this before, I thought, cotton-mouthed miserable, and then, once I got started, I felt great. I'd be all right this time, too.

"Mr. Stein can see you now," the receptionist said.

I clutched the guitar-case handle and walked stiff-legged toward the desk. I felt Michael take my free hand and squeeze it. His felt warm, and I realized mine was

105

icy. I held on tight. Dear God, I thought, make me
perfect

"Second door to your right," she said.

"Good luck," Michael whispered.

"Break a leg," I whispered back.

As we went into the office, I pulled my hand away. It
wouldn't help for us to come on like Hansel and Gretel.

"Hello, Michael and—Linda Ann Garcia, right?"

Dan Stein looked colorless, pale, with sparse graying
hair. I didn't know what I had expected, but not this
ordinary-looking middle-aged man.

"Sit down, kids. Just relax for a minute."

He swiveled in his chair behind the desk.

"Do you want to tell me what you've done; have you
had any experience?"

Michael's voice exuded confidence. "Well, we're just
getting started. We've done some local showcases
and . . ." A lie, but it sounded plausible.

Dan Stein nodded and smiled agreeably, and it was
then that I noticed his eyes. Small, blue, penetrating—
they flicked at Michael and then at me, sizing me up.

Michael talked some more, and Mr. Stein asked him
about his parents, friendly small talk. I had nothing to
say. I watched Mr. Stein's face. His casual, relaxed man-
ner almost covered the alert intelligence of his eyes.

"You have something prepared?"

"Yes," Michael said, "we thought we'd do 'Wild
Horses,' if that's okay."

"Fine," he said, "whenever you're ready."

We clattered guitar-case locks and took our guitars
out.

"We'll take just a minute to tune up," I said. I think
those were the first words I said beyond hello.

"Take your time," he said. "Just jump in whenever
you're ready."

My E string was a little flat, so I fixed it. I plucked

each of my strings for Michael, and he made some quick adjustments.

This was it. I took a deep breath and looked at Michael. I nodded and we counted off together, silently, one, two, three . . . we were on. He played three chords, I started the melody, the introduction was going okay, then into the lyrics.

> *Graceless lady*
> *You know who I am*

He took the harmony, and I thought he was just a little bit off.

> *You know I can't let you*
> *Slide through my hands*

I looked at Mr. Stein. He was glancing at his desk pad. Wait, I thought, when I get to the break in the middle. . . .

> *Wild horses*
> *Couldn't drag me away*

Finally, we got to it. This is where I was going to do my flashiest hammers, pull-offs, throw everything in. I was getting into it, and then Michael hit a wrong note. Okay, Michael, keep on going. . . . Oh God, no! He was shook and he missed a couple of beats! It was all I could do to figure where he was and get back together with him again. It took all my concentration to carry Michael through the break. The song dragged. I felt enmeshed in Michael's wrong notes and missed beats. Finally, we got back to the lyrics. We limped through it. It was all over.

I looked up at Michael. He was smiling and winked at me. I couldn't believe it; he actually looked happy. Doesn't he know, I thought. How could he not know? I forced myself to look at Dan Stein. He looked professionally pleasant. We had wasted his time, but he was going to be polite.

"Thanks for stopping in, kids."

"Thank *you*, Mr. Stein," Michael said. He was still smiling, still exuding confidence. "Do you think there might be something for us?"

"Let me think about it." He was dismissing us. "Michael, be sure to say hello to your father."

"Yes, I will."

I bent down and put my guitar in the case. My face felt hot. I closed the case and scraped my knuckle against the lock. Tears came to my eyes, suddenly and unexpectedly. I blinked them back.

Michael was holding the office door open for me, ready to go. "Well, thanks again, Mr. Stein," he said.

"Thank you," I whispered, starting through the door. The big break, the main chance, and it was all over. We had messed up, Michael had messed up, and I'd never have a chance like this again.

"*Ciao*," Mr. Stein said, looking over some papers on his desk. His disinterest was obvious, and I couldn't blame him. He thought I was the worst kind of amateur, doing bad Rolling Stones imitations. I was better than that! I was!

I whirled around in the doorway.

"Please, Mr. Stein! I know that was terrible. I can do so much better than that! Could you give me just another minute? Please!" I blurted it all out, feeling like a jerk but unable to stop myself.

"Linda . . ." Michael said.

"Wait for me outside," I said.

"Linda, what are you—" He took my arm.

"Let go of me." I shook myself loose. "Just wait for me outside."

The expression on Michael's face reminded me of something, and I couldn't look at him. I kept my eyes on Mr. Stein and felt Michael's body brush against me as he went through the doorway.

Mr. Stein put his papers down reluctantly.

"Look," he said, "it isn't necessary. . . ."

"Please. Let me do my best, just once. Then I won't bother you." I sat down quickly, took my guitar out as fast as I could, before he could see me out.

I knew what I was going to do before I touched the guitar. It was going to be "Blues for Linda Ann."

The first five notes. Vibrato on the F. I felt engulfed by the dark sounds. I saw my whole gray life stretching out in front of me, no miracles, no lucky breaks. I reached for the G sharp. Suddenly I remembered where I had seen the expression on Michael's face before. It was the same hurt, bewildered look that Jeff Breslow had had so many months ago when I left him sitting all alone in the school cafeteria, so many lifetimes ago when Michael was new. I felt a great sadness. "Blues for Linda Ann" was saying it all.

I let the last note reverberate and fade away. Then I looked up at Mr. Stein.

His eyes had come alive.

"Good," he said. He was looking me over, giving me his full attention. "What was that piece?"

" 'Blues for Linda Ann.' "

"Is that your own?"

"Yes," I said without skipping a beat. It was, really. Silk Garcia had meant it for me.

"Interesting. I'd like to hear you try that first number again, the one you did with Michael."

" 'Wild Horses'?"

"Yes."

I did the opening chords, Michael's part, and then I played the melody.

> *I have found my freedom*
> *But I don't have much time. . . .*

The break went well. I went all out, showing off as much technique as I could. Then I sang the chorus again.

> *Wild, horses*
> *Couldn't drag me away. . . .*

The tears I had been holding back came now. My voice was husky, but my fingering was impeccable. I was looking straight at Mr. Stein. The song wasn't about Michael anymore. It was about making it and not letting anything block me. Something like that, anyway. My feelings were too jumbled, and I wasn't sure of why I was crying.

> *Wild horses*
> *Couldn't drag me away*
> *Wild, wild horses*
> *We'll ride them someday. . . .*

"That was beautiful," Mr. Stein said. "How old are you?" I hesitated.

"The truth, please."

"I'll be sixteen next month."

I brushed the tears away with the back of my hand. He reached into a desk drawer and handed me a tissue. He watched me silently for a moment.

"I'm assuming your partnership was just dissolved?"

"Yes," I said.

"Very nice kid, Michael. Very nice kid, very nice family, but he's no help to you."

"I know."

"That first composition was extraordinary. . . . All right, here's our problem. I book acts for the concert circuit and for that I need names. So that's out. I also book for clubs, and you could be right for one of the smaller ones. You'd need a showcase, but—and here's the big but—no place is going to touch you before you're eighteen."

"Oh." So there would be nothing, after all.

"Don't look so unhappy. You're very talented. I think you have a unique quality, and I'm too busy to say things like that just to be nice. I'll remember you, and I'll remember your name. Linda Ann Garcia. Spend the next couple of years picking up as much experience as you can and then come and see me again. My office will be open to you."

"Thank you."

"You know, there's nothing wrong with being young. Take your time and build up a repertoire."

"I'll try."

"Linda Ann Garcia. Don't worry, I'll remember you."

I believed him. It wasn't going to be a miracle and it wasn't going to be Cinderella, but I believed him and I'd be back.

This time he got up from his chair and walked me to the door. He smiled at me and I smiled back. For the first time, I felt the man's warmth.

"You really are good. I'm sorry I can't do more for you now."

"Thank you, thank you so much, Mr. Stein," I said, meaning it, feeling aglow.

I was relieved to see Michael in the reception room. I wasn't sure he would be there. I was feeling so up, I wanted so badly to tell him what Mr. Stein had said, but his face was grim.

111

"I'm sorry, Michael, thanks for waiting, I just had to . . ."

Michael's strides were large, and I had difficulty keeping up with him. Finally he stopped in front of the elevators. He punched the down button.

"Michael—"

"What was that shit? That's all I want to know. I just waited around to ask you, exactly what was that?"

"I had to ask for another chance, it was so bad and I—"

"The hell it was, there was nothing wrong with it."

"Oh, Michael, we were terrible."

"Stein's a professional; he understands a little nervousness; he knows enough to discount it. What were you trying to do, promote your own personal—"

The elevator stopped and there were other people in it. He didn't look at me the whole way down. On the street, he was walking so fast, I almost had to run to stay at his side.

"We were supposed to be partners, remember? That was the deal, remember?"

"Oh, Michael, that sounds like an old MGM musical."

"What did he say to you?"

"He liked me; he really liked me; he said he'd remember me. He told me to come back when I'm eighteen. He said I had a unique quality."

"Congratulations."

"He meant it."

"Yeah, great. You got your introduction, right? I know when I've been had."

"Had?"

"Had. Used. Lady, you are an A1 user."

"What are you talking about?"

"You know what I'm talking about. I got you the introduction to Dan Stein. I got you the hairdo. Anything else I can do for you?"

112

I stopped short. He kept on walking without me and stopped at the car, parked halfway down the block. I didn't know if he was going to wait for me or not.

I rushed to catch up to him. "Look, you don't have to drive me home or anything. I just want to tell you something. The hairdo had nothing to do with it, nothing. Mr. Stein couldn't have cared less. He thought I was *good*. And don't worry, I'll pay you back for the haircut. I said I would."

"Forget it," Michael said, "that's not the point. Get in the car, I'll drive you home."

I got in. Neither of us said a word. He didn't so much as glance at me. I scrunched against the door on my side, watching Lexington Avenue pass by. There was an endless stretch of car seat between us. Was it yesterday, was it last week, that we always sat as close to each other as anatomically possible?

The car rattled across the Fifty-ninth Street Bridge and into Queens. The silence felt hostile, and it made my throat ache. At the same time, I couldn't help thinking about Mr. Stein. He had taken me seriously.

We were on the expressway before Michael finally spoke.

"Jesus! 'Wait outside for me! Let go of me!' What the hell was that?"

"Michael, I had to—"

"Right. I got you into Stein's office, so then you were on your own. Smooth move."

"You were making all those mistakes, and we were terrible. It was too important to me; can't you understand? I couldn't let a chance like that go. . . ."

"Shit, anybody can make a mistake. Stein knows that."

"You weren't good enough." My voice was very low. He looked straight ahead at the road, and I wasn't sure if he had heard me.

113

"All right, I should have practiced," he said finally.

I was startled. Was that it, the secret behind the no-effort nonchalance that I had loved so much? If you don't try too hard, you can never really fail?

"Michael," I said, "even if you didn't take the SATs, that's not so important. You can still take it next fall; you can still apply. . . ."

"I took the SATs last week," he said. "I did all right."

"You did what? You did what? You were just playing games, right? You were going on to Dartmouth or whatever, anyway, right?"

"Just for something to fall back on."

"I have nothing to fall back on! I was serious!"

"Don't worry," he said, "you'll do fine. Takers always do."

We went the rest of the way in silence. Expressway, North Bay Boulevard, Main Street. It was endless.

"You know, it wasn't my fault," I said. "What are you so mad about? You were dragging *me* down."

"Man, that was some ride you took me on," he said.

"What? What are you talking about?"

"You held out and you held out until I told you I knew Dan Stein. And then Open Sesame. There's a name for that."

"It wasn't like that! Damn you, you know that's not true!" If we hadn't been in traffic, I think I would have hit him. I badly wanted to punch him.

He pulled to the curb in front of my house. He didn't even put the car in Park; he had the motor running with his foot on the brake, waiting for me to get out.

I wouldn't have felt as bad if there had been a last speech, something signifying regret, lost love, something bittersweet.

All he said was "See you" and drove off.

12

I took off the white Lees and hung them over a chair. I took off my white shirt and found my old blue terry-cloth bathrobe. I wrapped it around and tied it tight for comfort. I didn't want to think about Michael yet. I was hollow inside. Everything would have been all right if only I had left Dan Stein's office with him. If I hadn't been so . . . But then Dan Stein would never have heard me. I should have been happier about that part of it, but it was like winning a prize and having no one to show it to. I had Dan Stein's words to hug myself, and I was all alone. Someday, though, I'd be back at his office to get a real job and . . . It didn't make me feel any better.

When the telephone rang, at first I thought it might be Michael, and I rushed into the kitchen to answer it. Then, even as I was reaching for the receiver, I knew it wouldn't be. There was no way we could roll everything back to last week. There was nothing I wanted to say to him now, anyway.

"Hello."

"Hello. Could I speak to—uh—Linda Garcia, please?"

"This is Linda."

"Oh, hi. This is Marvin Breslow."

"Who?" I was twisting the end of the terry-cloth belt around my finger.

"Marvin Breslow. Jeff's cousin."

Jeff's cousin? Why in the world would a cousin of Jeff's . . . ?

"Jeff asked me to check out some records for you."

"Oh, yes!" The intern at Beth Israel!

"Sorry it took me so long to get back to you. Things get pretty frantic around here."

"Yes, I know."

"You're Jeff's girl friend, right?"

I paused. "Sort of." Was that the way Jeff had seen it?

"See, Jeff didn't tell me. What's your connection with this Garcia? What did you want to know?"

I couldn't miss the caution in his voice.

"Silk Garcia . . . I mean, Antonio Garcia . . ." I began. Obviously our last names were the same. I didn't know what to say. This time I wanted to hear unedited truth.

"Right, Antonio Garcia. That's what I've got here."
There was a silence. It was my turn.

"Antonio Garcia . . . He was a very distant relative of my father's, fourth cousin removed, something like that. Well, we heard he had died, and the family just wanted to know what happened. Jeff said you could probably check the hospital records for us."

"Your family wasn't in touch with him?"

"No, I never even met him. I'm not sure that my parents ever did; he was related to my father's stepfather, something like that; it was very distant, not even a blood relative. I don't think. . . ." I forced myself to stop, and I took a breath. I hoped I wasn't laying it on too thick.

"You never even met him?"

116

"No. We just thought we'd like to know about him, I mean, what happened to him."

"As long as you're not emotional about him or anything . . ."

"No, no, not at all." My voice was wonderfully cool.

"Okay, this is what I've got. Antonio Garcia. The immediate cause of death was hepatitis. God knows how long he'd been walking around with it. He was unconscious when they brought him into Emergency. Let's see, that was January 5. He died January 6."

"Hepatitis?"

"The body was in terrible condition. Odd thing, when he came in, the examining doctor put down his age as approximately sixty. Then, when his friend claimed the body, it turned out he was only thirty-eight. Isn't that something?"

"How could a doctor make a mistake like that?"

"Oh, it was a natural mistake. The body was a mess. He was a drinker; his liver was shot. It's amazing that he lasted as long as he did. On top of everything else, he was an addict."

"An addict?"

"Needle tracks all over both arms and legs, some of them badly infected. He must have been running out of veins."

"Oh."

"I guess that about covers it."

"Who claimed the—claimed his body?"

"Wait a minute, I've got it down here someplace . . . Raymond Bronson. No indication here of any family."

"He was very distant. . . ."

"Yeah, well, I didn't think there'd be much connection between this guy and a girl friend of Jeff's. I hope this won't upset anybody in your family."

"No. No."

"Okay, then."

117

"Was there anything else? On the records?"

"No, just male, Caucasian, blood type A, hair black, eyes gray. That's about it."

"Thank you."

"Tell Jeff I finally called, okay?"

"Yes, I will."

"How're the parakeets doing? Any word from the Science Search?"

"What? No, I don't think so."

"Tell the little genius I'm rooting for him. I'll come by if I ever get a couple of days off."

"Yes. Thank you."

"That's okay. . . . Well, so long."

"So long."

I sat down on the kitchen stool.

I tried to sort it out in my mind, tried to get past the words, tried to see Silk Garcia.

I think I had half-expected something like this. It all fit, all of Bronson's talk about the nighttime world, Mom's and Grandma Quinn's secrecy, Marvin Breslow's words. "Whatever else he was." "The body was a mess." A man with gray catlike eyes. "Needle tracks all over both arms and legs." An abused body. An abused talent stuck in a stage show band, staring out at the audience. A man wheeling a baby carriage, nodding to the neighbors and asking about colic. "Silk Garcia, going straight." A man going through hard times with a cheerleader for a wife.

Mom, the cheerleader. Did his troubles start after she left him? Was he too sensitive? Taking his kid away must have been the final blow. Was that when he turned to drugs and liquor? Jeanne Garcia née Jeanne Quinn. I could imagine it. When the musician's life wasn't so glamorous, the beautiful blonde from North Bay caved in.

I wanted to cry for him, but I couldn't. I couldn't cry on that other day, either, the day she told me he was dead.

When Mom came home, I couldn't talk at all, and she was too tired to notice. Her lines looked deeper than usual. I had a mix of feelings, a rush of caring because she looked so worn out and, at the same time, hard anger. She should have stood by him and she didn't. Instead, she went right back to North Bay, scene of her triumphs, only this time, she was saddled with Silk Garcia's kid. Did she feel guilty every time she looked at me? Was that why she wouldn't talk about him? No wonder she couldn't listen to "Blues for Linda Ann."

We had spaghetti, and she ate with her elbow on the table. How many times had she said, when I was little, "Mabel, Mabel, get your elbows off the table." And all those other mother-things. "Look both ways, very, very carefully, when you cross Main Street." The year I was a princess for Halloween, she had spent the whole night before sewing on pink sequins for me; it was the prettiest thing I had ever seen. And yet . . .

"You're not eating. What's the matter?"

"Nothing."

"How was school today?"

"Okay."

She poured Pepsi into her glass.

"It was one of those days, everybody trying things on and nobody buying." A deep sigh. It didn't call for an answer, and I didn't want to talk to her.

"Pass the salt, Linny."

Her chin line was getting soft and she looked weak, I thought. Too weak to have been proud of Silk Garcia's lookalike in front of Grandma. And weak enough to have destroyed Silk Garcia.

"What's the matter with you, Linny?"

"Nothing."

"You look so strained. Do you feel all right?"

"Yes."

"Wait a minute. Weren't you going to have dinner with Michael tonight? In the city?"

"Well, something came up."

"Why didn't you have dinner with Michael?"

"All right. I'm not going out with him anymore."

"Oh, honey, everyone has fights sometimes. That's not so serious. Why don't you just go right over to the phone and apologize and make up and—"

"No."

"Linda, don't let bad feelings go on. Call him right now and—"

"Why do you want me to call him? You don't even know what we had a fight about. Why are you so sure I should apologize?"

"Linda, Michael is so special. Such a nice family and everything; you don't meet someone like that every day. Don't throw it away."

I stared at her. "You don't even know his family. So please leave me alone."

She looked at me and her voice went dead. "Fine," she said, "suit yourself. Make your own mistakes."

The rest of the meal was silence. Some set of values, I thought. Of course, she had an affinity to the golden boy from Ocean Point. I had a flash that had she known about us together in the apartment all those afternoons, she wouldn't have minded too much. What mistakes was she thinking of? My father? Me?

"Clear the table and wash up, Linda. I've got to get off my feet."

I sponged the dishes and watched the soap bubbles. Some popped. Some floated up above the sink for a little while. I tried to watch the soap bubbles keep the words out of my mind. "The body was in terrible condition. . . . claimed the body. . . . The body was a mess. . . ."

He sounded so alone, so bruised. My father who made such beautiful music. It hurt me so much. Maybe if he had received love to match all the love, all the longing that was in "Blues for Linda Ann," maybe it would have been different. I heard the echo of myself talking to Marvin Breslow. ". . . It was very distant, not even a blood relative, I don't think. . . ." "I'm sorry," I whispered, "I had to say that, I didn't mean to deny you." Flesh and blood. He would be part of me forever. She should have helped him. She should have let me help him. Or at least try.

"Lin," she called from the living room, "there's a good movie on."

I put a glass in the dishrack. Why didn't she at least let him have some contact with me?

"Come watch, it's a golden oldie. . . ."

I had to scrub hard with Brillo to get the remnants of sauce off the spaghetti pot. Why did she just wipe him out of my world, as if he had never existed?

"Ginger Rogers and Fred Astaire. . . ."

"Not now," I called back.

For some reason, the punch line of a joke that Bubbles had told one night, a joke I couldn't even remember, came into my mind.

"What do I call you now that 'mother' is a dirty word?"

13

Spring in North Bay is so beautiful that it's unreal. Lloyd Hill Road becomes a mist of pink and white azaleas and dogwoods. All this time, I had been rushing up Lloyd Hill Road on my way to school, too wrapped up in Michael and myself to even notice. Now that I was feeling so sad, I was aware of all the incredible beauty surrounding me, and it weighed me down.

I wondered if the damp-earth smell of May was a subliminal mating scent or if school had always been like this. Peter O'Connell and Chrissie Moore were melting together at the second-floor lockers. On the stairs down to the gym, there were two kids I didn't know, locked together and oblivious to my almost stepping on them. All through the halls, hands clasped, arms around waists, two by two. It made my throat hurt.

Out of habit, I looked for a glimpse of the sandy-gold hair. When I did see him, in the hall after Spanish, that familiar feeling washed over me. He looked at me from a great distance, as if I were someone he just vaguely remembered, and nodded in my general direction. The slightest nod possible, barely moving his chin. I wondered if someday I would see him and feel absolutely nothing. Or would the sight of hair that particular color, even on a stranger, even years from now, still make my breath catch?

Lunch was the worst. I was invisible.

The table was crowded as usual. Jan, Beverly, Ron Gilroy, Michael's arm thrown around Bubbles, Sonny, everyone. I hesitated in the aisle for just a moment before I moved on. It was Michael's crowd; it had never been mine.

The cafeteria was full of kids, yelling, laughing, rushing to tables, saving seats. I saw Jeff at a corner table with some people from the Science Department. I wanted to tell him about the phone call from his cousin, but he seemed deep in conversation.

"Watch it!"

The corner of a tray grazed my arm. I moved out of the way and finally found an empty chair. Eating, that first day, was very much like chewing rubber.

Every spring the Guidance Department at North Bay High School has evening meetings with small groups of parents to discuss program planning for next term and things like that. Mom got a notice for the sophomore parents' meeting, last names *E* through *G*.

She was eating dinner with one eye on the clock, and she seemed very pressured about it, so I said, "You don't really have to go, Mom."

"I think it's important."

"It's only about the courses I'll be taking next year. I know just about everything I want to take, anyway."

"I want to hear what they say," Mom said. "Your junior year is very important."

The meeting was at 8:00 P.M. and Mom started getting ready at 7:00. I sat cross-legged on my bed and watched her. I didn't think any other mother was going through all those preparations just for the Guidance Department. First, she brushed her hair and rolled it carefully into a French knot. It looked fine, but she took it down and brushed again and started all over. She began her makeup, and her equipment made a pile on the dresser. She bent over and peered into the mirror and worked on her eyes. Two colors of shadow and outliner and eyebrow pencil and mascara and highlighter . . . Good God, even the eyelash curler! It must have been hard for her each time she went back into North Bay High School. Jeanne Quinn returns to scene of former triumphs.

"How do I look?"

"Fine, Mom, it's only a guidance meeting."

She put on a black dress with a matching jacket and brushed off imaginary lint. She looked too elaborate. She stood very stiffly and hesitated at the door before she left.

"Well, so long," she said, her hand on the knob.

"So long, Mom."

"Well . . . I'll be back soon."

I wandered around the apartment for a while, and then I spread the newspaper on the table and checked the TV listings. Nothing much to see. I turned some pages. I skimmed through the movie ads. Concerts ads. The name "Lonigan" caught my eye. The Johnny Lonigan Quintet at the Yellow Door on MacDougal Street. The Johnny Lonigan Quintet. That was the group Silk Garcia had played with. They were there, in the flesh, just a few miles away right now, but Silk Garcia was gone forever. The sadness felt like an old, dull ache.

I tried to practice the guitar for a while, but the notes were just black dots on lined paper. Johnny Lonigan. I wondered what he could tell me.

I gave up on practicing. I just played distractedly, pieces that I had learned long ago. After a while, I felt a lot better and I was really getting into "Stairway to Heaven" when Mom came in.

"How was it?"

"Mr. Reid was very nice."

"He is," I said. "All the kids like him."

"Sit down over here on the couch, Lin." She kicked off her shoes. "We have a lot to talk about."

"Why? What did he say?"

"Nothing about you personally. He talked to the whole group. Come on, sit down here."

I reluctantly put down my guitar. I was in no mood for mother-daughter conversations. I sat down next to her and waited.

"Well," she said, "the junior year is really important. Up till now, it's been mostly required courses, right?"

"Right."

"But now, you have all kinds of choices open to you."

"I know, Mom. Mr. Reid talks to the kids, too."

"You could take business courses, typing and shorthand and things like that so you'll always be able to . . ."

Typing and shorthand? Me? She went on and on and I listened intermittently.

"Mr. Reid said . . . Accounting and Business English . . . on the other hand, there's no reason you can't go on to college . . . financial aid . . . commuting distance and . . . part-time job. . . . It would be so nice if you could be a schoolteacher . . . academic requirements . . . and then in your senior year . . ."

She was planning out a whole life, years and years of a life. Not mine.

"Well, what do you think?" she said. "You have a choice to make."

"Mom, I could have saved you the trip. I told you I know just about everything I want to take next year."

"What?"

"Music Theory 1 and History of Music next year.

Then Music Theory 2 in my senior year. Pat says I need to know more theory. . . ."

"What are you talking about?"

"That's about all that North Bay offers. I'll go on at the Guitar Institute, of course, and—"

"Just forget about this guitar nonsense. You have some serious decisions to make."

"I *have* made a serious decision. I'm a musician. I've told you that."

"Linda, we need to make practical plans for—"

"Listen to me for a minute, Mom. I went to see a man—"

"Mr. Reid said that if you take—"

"Mom, listen, please. I went to see a man named Dan Stein. Maybe you've never heard of him, but a lot of people have."

"Who? No, I've never heard of him."

"Mom, listen, a lot of people can't even get to see him, can't even get a foot in his door, but I did, because of Michael. I auditioned for him, and he thought I was good. Really, he did. Maybe someday I'll get a job through him, but anyway, he thought I was good and he *knows*. I do have a chance."

I thought she might look at least a little bit happy for me, but it was like that time way back in third grade when Miss Cornell said I was musically talented.

"You had no right to do that! You had no right to go running around to auditions without my permission!"

"Mom, aren't you glad that I was good enough to—"

"Good enough for what? To spend your life in gin mills? I won't allow it!"

Here I was, finally sharing my good news with someone, and she was turning it into nothing.

"You won't allow it?" I stood up and my voice was loud and harsh. "You can't 'not' allow it! I *am* a musician! Just like my father! Just like him."

126

"Stop it! You're nothing like him!"

"I am! I am like him! I even look like him. I am just exactly like him. I could be his twin!"

"You're not at all. . . ."

"Why? Because he was a junkie and a drunk?" I used those words, straight out, no softening them. Maybe if I got used to saying it straight out, it would stop hurting so much after a while. I watched her eyes widen.

"Yes, I know," I said. "My God, there was so much more to him than that!"

"So much more to him? Really?" Her lips were a tight line, and the skin was white around the perimeter of the bright red lipstick.

"How could you be so dumb?" I said. "How could you not appreciate . . . ?"

"You and your father! You don't know anything! You don't know what you're talking about!" She stood up and faced me. The tone of her voice and the look on her face should have warned me to stop.

"You were too dumb to understand—" I yelled.

That's when she slapped me. She really swung back and hit me hard. My cheek was stinging. I had never been slapped before. My cheek was red-hot and stinging. I turned and walked out and slammed the front door behind me.

Main Street was dark and almost deserted. Some of the stores had night lights in the windows, pale and blue. There was jukebox music coming out of the Emerald Isle bar. Everything else was dark. Even Gino's Pizza was closed. I walked toward the Boulevard and my cheek was still warm. I would have liked someone's arm around me. I would have liked someone walking with me, just quietly, understanding. There was no one, and I had nowhere to go.

Then I was walking along Lloyd Hill Road. It had no

streetlights, and the night was black and velvet soft. I turned a corner and took deep breaths of the May scents. Somehow, I found myself in front of Jeff Breslow's house. I don't think I had meant to go there.

On impulse, I rang the bell.

Mrs. Breslow answered. She looked surprised, but she gave me that big, toothy smile and suddenly it seemed warm and comforting.

"Why, Linda! Hello, how are you, dear?"

"Fine, thanks, Mrs. Breslow." I was really glad to see her. "Is Jeff home?"

"Yes, he's in the Bird Room. Go on in."

I went through the living room, with its bright orange carpeting. Everything was so familiar. I was eager to see Jeff and talk to him, maybe that whole innocent time could come back again. I rushed right into the Bird Room and Jeff was there and Sam was flying around and . . . Janet Craig.

There was a silence and Jeff looked at me, surprised.

"Hi, Jeff," I said.

"Oh . . . hi, Linda," he said. His whole face was a question. "Do you know Janet Craig? Linda Garcia . . ."

Janet was a senior, and I had seen her around. She had stringy pale blond hair and a sharp-looking face: pointed nose, pointed chin. I didn't like her. She stood next to Jeff and twined her arm around his. She was making a point of it.

"Oh, yes, Linda," she said. "Jeff has mentioned you. . . ." She let it hang in the air.

"Uh . . . we were just doing the cages," Jeff said. "Remember Sam?"

"Of course. Oh—what's happening with the Science Talent Search?"

Another small silence. "That was over a while ago," Jeff said.

"Oh," I said. "I'm sorry. I didn't know."

128

"I got an Honorable Mention."

"I'm sorry, Jeff."

"That's okay," he said. "My project wasn't that great. Next year's will be a lot better."

"Oh."

"Janet did a study on embryonic development that was fantastic." He was beaming with pride and put an arm around her. "She got Third Prize. Now she's working in electronics, working with really sophisticated alarms that may have enormous commercial potential. We're still experimenting, though, and . . ." He started to laugh and she joined in. ". . . and right now, her mother can't enter the laundry room except between one and three without an alarm going off." They were laughing hard. It was like a family joke, and I smiled politely.

"Well, I was just passing by," I said, "and I stopped in to say hello."

"I'm glad you did, Lin," Jeff said. His face was earnest and kind.

"Well, I have to be going," I said.

He turned to Janet. "I'll walk Linda to the door. Be right back."

"Okay," she said. Her hand on his arm looked possessive. "Come right back."

Jeff stood outside the front door with me, next to the big rhododendron. It was covered with white blooms now.

"Lin, I'm glad you and Janet had a chance to meet. She's very special."

"I'm glad, too." I wished I thought Janet was more appealing.

"She's wonderful, Lin. I hope you'll get to know her."

"I'm sorry I dropped in like that," I said, "without any warning."

129

"That's okay. . . . Lin, is anything wrong?"

"No, no, I'm fine."

"Is everything all right?"

"Oh, sure," I said. "I have to go. So long, Jeff." I started down the path and then I turned back. "Jeff, I just want you to know. I think you're a terrific person. I just wanted to tell you that. And I'm sorry."

He looked puzzled. "Lin, we'll talk sometime, okay? I kind of have to get back to Janet."

"Sure, Jeff. So long."

I walked back to Main Street. A train had just come in and a few late straggling commuters were coming from the station. I walked along aimlessly for a while. I was glad for Jeff. I truly was. He deserved to have someone feel about him the way Janet obviously did.

I went home again. Because I had nowhere else to go.

When I came in, Mom was sitting on the couch in the same spot she had been before. She had her hands clasped loosely in her lap, and she was looking down at them. I took a step into the living room and she looked up. She looked embarrassed. I looked away. I felt embarrassed, too.

Finally, she said, "I shouldn't have slapped you."

"I know," I said.

"You provoked it, though."

I started into the bedroom.

"Wait."

I turned in the doorway. There was a long, awkward silence.

"How long have you known about him?"

"About a week."

"Who? How did you . . .?"

"An intern at Beth Israel Hospital."

"I didn't want you to know."

"It's all right," I said.

"No one should have—"

"It's not the end of the world, Mom. I know other things about him, too. More important things. I know how great he was. He was a genius. He was a really great musician. Maybe if you had stood by him just a little longer, helped him . . ."

"That's really something." Her mouth curled. "How did you ever get so hung up on him?"

"You should have told me about him. Why didn't you ever tell me? You and Grandma—you made me feel ashamed of myself because I was like him. You made me feel like he was nothing, like there was something wrong with me. Too bad I didn't get born looking like a Quinn, you know?"

"Linda, I didn't . . . I know Grandma is kind of . . . I was always proud of you. I never meant to—"

"Oh, come on, I couldn't even ask a simple question about him without you freezing. There were so many wonderful things about him that you could have told me. Knowing the bad stuff is all right. It just makes me sad for him. But knowing how talented and special he was makes up for it. It makes me feel special; it makes me feel proud of myself; it gives me something to live up to. You had no right to deprive me of all that. You had no right to keep him from me all those years."

"Don't, Linda." Her voice seemed shaky. "Don't, honey."

"What?"

"That's some fantasy you've got there. Don't get caught up in a fantasy like that. You don't know anything about him." She took a deep breath, and I could see her willing her mask back into place. "All right. I shouldn't have slapped you. I'm sorry about that and that's all." She was up and moving. "I'm going to clean up the kitchen, and we'll talk about your next year's program another time."

131

"Mom!" I rushed across the room and took her arm. "Talk to me now. What don't I know? Mom, look at me. What else is there?"

"Nothing. There's nothing else."

I was still holding her arm, stopping her from going into the kitchen. "Tell me about him."

"I have nothing to tell you." She wouldn't look at me.

"Why did you slap me, Mom? Just because I said you didn't appreciate him?"

"You called me dumb and I . . ." She was flustered and I was surprised to see her turning red.

"I don't even remember saying that."

"You called me dumb and I . . ." Her skin was so fair and the red was in distinct blotches. I had to strain to hear her. "Dumb. Beautiful but dumb. Not like her sister Katherine. Not college material, Grandma said. So I—"

"I didn't mean anything."

"When you said that word, it just got to me and—"

"Oh, Mom!"

"—and I don't go around slapping kids, I'm not like that."

"I know. It's all right."

"Grandma did that, you know, put people in tight little boxes. Katherine was the smart one, and I was the pretty one."

"Katherine told me about you," I said, "when you were in high school. She said you were so pretty and the boys followed you around and everything. It sure didn't sound like you were unhappy."

"I didn't know how to be anything but pretty. Everyone expected something of me, something special, but I didn't know how to *do* anything. I had no real plans for after graduation, and I was almost afraid to leave high school. How was I going to live up to that

132

golden-girl image?" She started to laugh, but it sounded wrong. "And then I met your father. The first time I ever saw him, he was wearing a red satin shirt, can you imagine . . . and he was in a New York City nightclub, for God's sake, and he was so full of life. He seemed so exciting and I got caught up in the bright lights and all that and . . . it was so thrilling and . . . I thought he was the answer for me."

"And he wasn't?"

"No."

"Why? What do you mean?"

She shook her head and didn't say anything.

"Wasn't there any way you could have helped him?"

"No. His problems went back long before I ever met him. You were a really cute little girl, you know. You could spell your name when you were two and you deserved as much of a chance as any other kid and—No, I couldn't help him. I could only have kept him company. But I loved you so much, and I had to come back to North Bay. I never meant to make you feel ashamed of yourself. Maybe I should have told you something about him, I don't know. . . . I wanted to forget about the time I was with him and . . ." Her voice trailed off.

"Was it that bad?"

"Yes," she said. "Yes, it was."

"Mom, I'm sorry." I put my arms around her.

"You're nothing like him," she said. "Not at all. Not in any way." She sounded as if she was trying to convince herself.

When we went to bed, I couldn't sleep. I stared up at the ceiling, not really seeing anything in the dark, listening to Mom breathing in the other bed.

"Couldn't you have let him see me, though? Just sometimes? Just for visits?"

133

"I had nothing to do with it." Her answer seemed strange, and I thought about it for a long time.

"What do you mean?" I said.

No answer.

"Mom," I said into the dark, "what else was there? What don't I know?"

I waited for an answer, but except for her breathing, there was no sound. I was sure she wasn't asleep. Her breathing was too jagged. I could almost feel her tensing up in the dark. I was about to ask again and then I didn't. Some long-ago memory was conjuring up too much pain for her.

I tried hard to remember him. Maybe just around the corner, past the next dark edge of my mind. . . . All I could come up with were the same things I had told Jeff in the school cafeteria so long ago.

"Sometimes I think I remember him."

"Do you?"

"Just vague things. I don't know if I really remember or if it's something I've dreamed."

"Like what?"

"Well, riding along on his shoulders and ducking under the awnings and laughing. And another thing. Hanging on to his arm with both hands and the smell of gasoline and a lot of loud voices."

"Is that all?"

"That's all."

Maybe Johnny Lonigan could fill in the blanks.

14

I called the Yellow Door twice before I reached Johnny Lonigan. When I finally spoke to him on the phone, I was surprised and pleased with myself. I'd had a rough idea of what I was going to say, but when I was actually talking to him, it came out so smooth. Some of Michael Harrison must have rubbed off on me. My name was Margaret Farlow, I was a graduate student at New York University, and I was doing a thesis on jazz guitarists. I wanted to interview him about Silk Garcia. When he started brushing me off, telling me he had nothing to say, no time, things like that, I didn't get all shy and quiet the way I would have just a few months ago.

"I'm really disappointed," I said easily, "because Ray Bronson told me to call you."

There was a silence at the other end and then "Ray Bronson? No kidding, Ray Bronson? Why me? Why would he want *me* to talk to you about Silk Garcia?"

And then he said I could come down and see him between sets at the Yellow Door. It had been that easy.

I picked a Thursday night, when Mom was working, so that I could get ready and leave while she was away.

I had said I'd be spending the evening studying late with a friend. I hope that Mom would be asleep when I got back so that I could get rid of the clothes and makeup without her seeing me. I had to look older. I found a black jacket and skirt of Mom's that fit well enough when I pulled the belt tight. I used her dark lipstick and then I fooled around with her eye stuff—liner and shadow and mascara. It only emphasized my eyes, though, and they looked as much like Silk Garcia's as ever. I tried sunglasses. Mom's were light green, not really that dark-looking, so maybe they wouldn't look too strange at night. The dark slash of mouth, the glasses, Mom's clothes did make me look unfamiliar. This time, no one would know I was Silk Garcia's kid.

It was dark out, but Sixth Avenue in Greenwich Village was a jumble of lights, people, full of activity. Neon daylight. I felt excited—because I was on my way to see Johnny Lonigan, because the streets around me were full of life, because Silk Garcia had lived here once with me and Mom. There were three men standing on the curb, trying to hail a cab. They were black and had long hair hanging down in ringlets. I guessed that they were Rastafarians. I had read about the pot-smoking religious cult in magazines and stuff. Everything was right there, in person, all around me.

MacDougal Street wasn't hard to find. It was narrow and curvy, and there was a store that sold handcrafted leather things and then—the Yellow Door. It had just that: a brightly painted yellow door. There was a long flight of stairs going down, and I could hear the music and smell the smoke before I entered the room. It was mirrored, cool and dimly lit, and for a moment I was disoriented. The mirrors and Mom's light green sunglasses. Was I looking at a bandstand or just a reflection? The bar was mirrored, too, and everything was elegant and shiny. The men in the band came into focus. A tall man with grayish-red hair, playing sax. That must be Johnny Lonigan, I thought. The music was slow, smoky, middle-of-the-night jazz. Sax, piano, guitar, drums, and bass. The Johnny Lonigan Quintet, ice cubes tinkling in glasses and the murmur of voices. I stood in a corner near the bar and waited. When the musicians straggled off the bandstand, I rushed over to the sax player."

"Hello, Mr. Lonigan?"

He nodded.

"I'm Margaret Farlow."

He just looked at me.

"I talked to you on the phone. About Silk Garcia."

"Oh yeah, right," he said. "Just a second."

He stopped a waiter. "Billy, bring me a burger in back, okay?" and then, to me, "Do you want something?"

"No, thanks," I said. I was afraid to order anything, wondering how much a hamburger would cost in a place like this.

"Okay, follow me. We can talk in the back."

He led me through a side door. The back of his hair was more gray than red, and his shoulder blades showed through his black dinner jacket. I followed him into what seemed to be a dressing room. There was a counter with a long mirror and stools in front of it. A bare light bulb with a cord hung from the ceiling. The walls had been painted green, but they were peeling in places and you could see yellow underneath. Here and there were bits of graffiti. I was surprised by the total contrast to the streamlined front room. He sat down on a stool and motioned me to sit down on one, too.

"So what's this all about?" he said. His voice was hoarse.

"Well, I'm doing my thesis on jazz guitarists, and since Silk Garcia played with you, I thought—"

"Why Garcia?" The harsh light threw dark shadows under his eyes.

"I have notes about Django Reinhardt and Charlie Christian," I said, "and finding out about Silk Garcia would round out—"

"Ray Bronson has tapes of Garcia. I don't have anything like that."

"I've heard them," I said. "What I need is the personal—uh, you know, about what he was like and . . ."

"Why bother with Garcia?"

"He was one of the greats," I said. I was careful to keep the pride out of my voice. "He was one of the greats and I wanted to find out about him. I mean, him as a person."

"Ray Bronson sent you, huh?"

"Yes, he did."

"That's a tough one to figure. Why would Bronson want me to . . . ?" He rubbed his chin. "Okay. Do you have a tape recorder?"

"Uh . . . no," I said "I'll just remember our conversation and maybe make some notes. . . . I've found that talking into a mike makes people too self-conscious." That sounded good, I thought. I had heard someone say that on TV.

"Yeah, that's true," he said. He coughed. "Okay, go ahead."

"I know Silk Garcia played with you for years," I said. "I don't want to start with specific questions. I thought maybe you could tell me some anecdotes or . . ."

"You want anecdotes about Silk Garcia?" He looked at me incredulously. I wondered if I had said something wrong.

The waiter came in and stepped into the silence between us. He put the plates and a bottle of beer on the

138

counter in front of Lonigan. The smell of hamburger and french fries made me hungry.

"Thanks, Billy. Listen, you sure you don't want something?"

"No, thanks."

"I didn't have time for dinner before and . . . look at least have the coleslaw, all right? I never eat it." He pushed the side order of coleslaw and a fork toward me and took a bite of the hamburger.

I started on the coleslaw. Eating together made things easier.

"Want a beer?" he said.

"No, thanks."

"What did Bronson tell you about Garcia?"

"Mostly about his music. He said he was one of the giants. You'd agree with that, wouldn't you?"

"Yeah," he said. "He was good."

"Well, can you tell me about him? As a person, not just as a musician?"

"I can't get over Bronson sending you. I guess he finally had enough. Okay, I guess he was ready to fill out the record." Another bite of hamburger. "I don't think any of this belongs in your thesis, though. Why don't you just stick to the music?"

"What do you mean?"

He looked at me pleasantly and dipped a french fry into the ketchup on his plate. "If you're talking about Silk Garcia, you're talking about a psycho. That has nothing to do with jazz. That has to do with sickness."

"What?"

"The son-of-a-bitch had a piece missing."

"Why are you saying that?" I said. "Look, I know about him. I know he was an alcoholic and an addict, but—"

"Yeah, that too," he said. "Sweetheart, if you want a

139

romantic story about your addict-musician, don't come to me for it. Make it up yourself."

"What do you mean, a piece missing?" I put down the fork. It clanked against the plate.

"He didn't have normal human feelings. All he did was use people up. He used them up and threw them away like some old crumpled gum wrapper."

"I don't understand."

"You know why they called him 'Silk,' don't you?"

"Because of the way he played," I said. "Smooth as silk."

"No. Because of the way he was. Slippery as."

"What?"

"Slippery as silk. A pathological liar. I don't care how good a musician he was, you ought to leave him out of your thesis and concentrate on Reinhardt, Christian, maybe McLaughlin. . . . That's not what you wanted to hear, is it?"

A piece of cabbage was stuck in my throat. "I want to hear the truth," I said.

"All right. Now look, I don't have an ax to grind. It was a long time ago, and he didn't do me in more than he did anyone else. Aside from not showing when I needed him. When I think of the gigs he screwed up for everybody. . . . but that's what you expect from a junkie, right? No, it was more than that. The son-of-a-bitch was a walking horror show."

I was turning cold, as if the air conditioning had suddenly gone on full blast.

"You want Silk Garcia anecdotes? There was the time Bronson and his lady took him in. Bronson left him alone there for a while and when he got back, he was cleaned out. Like Silk took cash, clothes, any damn thing he could carry out. This was *Bronson*, you know? You want more anecdotes? I had this young guitarist after I got rid of Garcia. This young kid, Tom Gaines was his name, idolized Silk. He was just starting out and he thought Silk was the greatest that ever lived. So when Silk came to him . . . He came to Tommy and said, 'Lend me your guitar, man, just for the night, I hocked mine and I got this gig, if you'd lend me yours, just for the night . . .' Tom was honored to help Silk out, right, only he had a record session that week so he told Silk to get it back to him the next day. . . . You got it, kid. Tom never saw his guitar. Silk sold it. You want to hear more Silk Garcia anecdotes?"

I tried to keep my voice even. "That's all because he was an addict, wasn't it? If he hadn't been . . ." I was shivering.

"He was a psycho. Other people just weren't real to him, you know? And he was an operator. He could always charm someone into doing something for him." He carefully wiped the ketchup from his mouth and crumpled the napkin. "He knew how he was *supposed* to feel and he'd do the act. Kind of fascinating to watch him." Lonigan smiled. "Now all this doesn't belong in your thesis. It belongs in some shrink's book."

"I think you're wrong! I know he had feelings, real feelings! That record he made, 'Blues for Linda Ann' . . . that had so much love and longing in it and—" I couldn't go on.

" 'Blues for Linda Ann' ? I don't know that one."

" 'Blues for Linda Ann.' On the Royal Roost label."

"Oh yeah, I know what you mean, that one!" He smiled at me. "Say, you've really done your research! Right, that was 'Strung Out Blues.' "

"What?"

"That was 'Strung Out Blues.' When he recorded it, they didn't want to go with that title. Too drug-oriented, I guess. Most of the time, they'd just tack a title on afterward, anyway. So he was trying to think of something else, fast, and they told him to make it a girl's name. 'Strung Out Blues,' yeah, that was one of his good ones. He was a damn good musician."

"Linda Ann was his daughter's name," I whispered.

"You know, I think it was!" He took a gulp of beer and nodded at me with approval. "I have to hand it to you, you really do your homework."

"Did you know his daughter? . . . His wife?"

"Sure, I knew his wife. Her name was Jeannie. I felt for that girl. She was nice, a really nice kid. Beautiful and young and radiant. By the time she left, she was—faded, all through. He did a number on her."

"Why did she leave him?"

He took another drink of beer. "I'd say she had an even dozen reasons for leaving. And the last one was a winner."

He stopped and he wasn't saying anything else. I could have gotten up then, thanked him and walked out. That's what I wanted to do. I didn't want to hear any more. I needed to be by myself. I needed to think about "Strung Out Blues." I didn't want to hear any more. But I stayed and stared at him and felt a presence heavy in the room. I couldn't stop now.

"What happened?" I said.

"Look, this doesn't need to go into your thesis."

"All right. What happened?" His eyes were brown and a little bloodshot, and I stared into them, unable to move.

"Because it's a little much even for Silk Garcia."

"What happened?"

"Okay. Silk was in bad shape around that time. I felt sorry for Jeannie. He'd clean out their apartment and take off and not even leave her milk money for the baby. She was borrowing all over the place, borrowed from me sometimes, and you could see it was killing her. He looked bad at that time. I don't know what-all he was on then. Anyway, she was at work that day, and

142

he took his daughter for a walk. He did that sometimes. He seemed to like her, like he'd be laughing and everything. Well, she was about two years old, and they were passing the Mobil station, the one on the corner, right off Sixth Avenue."

I saw my reflection in the mirror, frozen, in Mom's light green sunglasses.

"I guess she wanted a drink and there was a Coke machine at the station, so they stopped there. Andrew Starkey owns the station, and he was there that day and he said Silk didn't even have any change and he was really strung out and fumbling through his pockets. There was this out-of-town couple, getting gas, Illinois plates on the car, and they were standing there. They saw the little girl and the woman started ooh-ing and aah-ing about how cute she was. Jeannie tried to dress her real nice all the time. Anyway, this couple was making a fuss over the little girl and Silk was fumbling and half out of his mind and they were saying how cute she was and Silk offered them the kid for five hundred bucks."

I tried to shake my head, to make the words stop.

"They said okay, to see if he was serious, and then they had the guy at the station call the cops. The kid was screaming and hanging on to Silk's leg. The cops had to pry her loose, and they took Silk in and they called Jeannie at work—she was modeling in the garment center someplace—and Jeannie took the kid and went back home. Some small town on the Island, I think. She even had to borrow train fare from the guy at the luncheonette on Eighth Street. The kind of girl Jeannie was, he got a letter from her a couple days later, with the money and a thank you and . . ."

His mouth kept on moving. I could see his lips moving but I couldn't hear the words.

I remember going through the room with the mirrors and up the stairs.

I took the subway and the roar was like a distant hum. I sat and didn't look at the other people and I got off at Thirty-fourth Street. I went through to the Long Island Railroad and I think the corridor was crowded and I think someone brushed against me. On the train, the conductor took my ticket and said something to me. His voice was far away, as if I were hearing it from underwater. My body moved a little with the motion of the train. I don't remember getting off. I don't remember walking down Main Street. The stairs in the building were extra dark; maybe one of the bulbs had burned out. I felt the coleslaw start to rise in my throat. I made it into the apartment and to the bathroom. When I threw up, I could taste a sour version of each ingredient separately and distinctly: mayonnaise, cabbage, carrot, green pepper. When there was nothing left, my stomach still wouldn't stop heaving. I hung over the toilet, panting. I will never be able to eat coleslaw again.

I lay on the bed and from somewhere, I heard Mom's voice. I felt a dark stain inside me, growing and spreading the way an ink stain seeps slowly into a blotter. I gagged again.

15

The night went by and a day and then the week-end and I lay in bed, staring at shadow patterns on the ceiling. I sank into sleep. Mom talked to me and her voice sounded far, far away. I shut my eyes.

"What's wrong, Linda?" and "Are you sick? Should I call a doctor?"

"No," I mumbled. "I'm just tired. Let me sleep."

I slept through the nights and in the daytime, the room looked gray. I knew there was sunshine coming through the windows, but it looked like lines of gray light. Mom forced some toast on me. I ate, just so she'd leave me alone. I chewed. It had no taste. I swallowed.

"Linda, you don't have a temperature, but . . ." There was a high edge to her voice that cut through the fog. "Linda, what's wrong?"

"I'm tired."

My head sank deep into the softness of the pillow. If she would just leave me alone. If I could just sleep and stop hearing Lonigan's hoarse voice saying those words. . . . "A piece missing . . . slippery as . . . used people up . . ." That's what Michael had said, too. "Lady, you are an A1 user." I thought of Jeff and his

145

bird charts. Dominant and recessive genes. Blue feathers make blue feathers and green feathers make green. Like father, like son. Chip off the old block. Blood tells. Birds of a feather.

What else had Michael said? Did I really hold out and hold out until he said he knew Dan Stein? "There's a name for that." How easily and glibly had I lied, how many times? I closed my eyes and saw Jeff's face the day I left him sitting all alone in the cafeteria. Jeff, who had shared his lunches with me so that I could pay for G.I. How could I have gone to his house like that when I needed someone, thinking I could pick it up again as if nothing had changed? Cardboard people. No human feelings. Mom's swollen ankles actually revolted me. I was Silk Garcia's kid, all right, and all I wanted to do was sleep it off. I wanted to sink down and down until everything was obliterated.

Then there was a deep, rumbling voice, shaking me awake.

"Linda."

Ray Bronson was leaning over me. Ray Bronson, sitting on the edge of my bed.

"Lonigan called me," he said. "When you ran out like that, he wondered what was going on and he called me. I figured it was you."

"It was all true, wasn't it?"

"Yes," he said, "but so was the other part, the part I told you. That was true, too."

I tried to wave him away with my hand. "It doesn't matter."

"It does matter."

I closed my eyes. I was hollow inside.

"Linda! Listen to me!"

I turned away from him, toward the wall. I curled myself tight under the blanket, my knees pulled up against my chest. I wanted his voice to fade away.

"Linda, everything I told you about him . . ."

"No," I said. "No more."

His hand was on my shoulder. I could feel his grip digging in through my blue cotton pajamas.

"Linda, listen."

I tried to curl myself tighter, but his huge hand was covering my shoulder, forcing me awake, turning me around to face him.

"He had no feelings," I said. "He was a liar. He was a psycho. He was a—"

"Of course he had feelings. You can't hear his music and not know that."

"He was a user. He was a—"

I saw myself that day with Michael, that day in Dan Stein's office. I saw myself shoving him aside. I remembered how I had felt at that moment—fierce, wild. I thought I loved him, but at that moment I could have run over him like a bulldozer.

Bronson was still talking. "Of course he had feelings, but he couldn't . . . connect . . . with anyone. Linda, he was a man in a cage. The only way he could express anything was through his music."

"I don't want to hear about him."

"He was screaming from inside his own prison. Listen to his music."

"No."

"Linda, he was just a man, you know?"

I propped myself up on my elbow. "How could you have been his friend? How could you?"

"He was a genius. I wanted to help him."

"He hurt everybody."

"He did try. He tried very hard to fill the role of husband and father, the way he thought it was supposed to be. . . ."

"He sure didn't make it."

"He did try. He wanted to be like everyone else."

147

"I hate him. I hate everything about him. I don't want any part of him."

"Whatever happened was a long time ago," he said quietly. I smelled the candy mints on his breath. "It's all over. Silk Garcia is gone."

"No," I said. "Not quite." I clenched my teeth to keep my lips from shaking.

"What?"

"Because I'm just exactly like him."

"What are you saying?"

"Step right up, folks, here's Silk Garcia all over again."

"I don't understand."

"But how can I go through a whole lifetime with a piece missing? It goes along with the gray eyes, you know, Linda Ann Garcia, the walking horror show."

"So that's what you've been thinking, lying there all this time?"

"Leave me alone," I said. I let my head sink back into the pillow and closed my eyes. "I don't want to talk."

"What do you know about him or his life?" The voice was low but insistent, coming at me again. "He came up all alone in a twisted nighttime world. You never paid his dues. There's no way you're Silk Garcia."

"Go away. I don't want to hear about him."

He stood up and the bed creaked as his weight was lifted from it.

"Fine," he said, "Fine, let's talk about Jeanne instead." His voice was still low, but I could hear an edge of anger. "Jeanne was just a kid herself then, but all she cared about was protecting you, hanging in there, doing her best. Now you've lived with her all your life. You're telling me that she never even made a dent? You're saying that everything she put into you didn't amount to a thing? You're one hundred percent Silk and zero Jeanne, huh?"

"You don't know the way I am."

"Something has got to come from her. And Jeanne was never one to lay around whimpering and feeling sorry for herself. She always showed class."

I sat up. "I'm not feeling sorry for myself! I'm facing the truth! There are things I've done. . . ."

"So you've done something. So you're feeling bad about something. Well, whatever you do, good or bad, it's all yours, girl. Don't lay it on Silk Garcia."

"I don't want any part of him! I don't want his talent either. I want nothing from him."

"Oh?" Bronson's eyebrows lifted. "Whatever made you think you had his talent?"

"I can play 'Blues for . . . Strung Out Blues,' all right?" Was he needling me? "I can play it note for note, exactly the way he did."

"Congratulations. You can do technical tricks and good imitations."

"I sound just like him." I was surprised that my face was getting warm. I was surprised to be feeling anything.

"It was *his* music, *his* style, *his* life. That still leaves you a long, long way to go. You're not Silk Garcia, no way."

I looked at him. His eyes were deep black velvet.

"You can't claim his accomplishments or his failures. You're not Silk Garcia, one way or the other. You're worried about something you've done? That's a great big difference right there. Silk wouldn't have worried about it."

I looked away.

"Look, he hit lower lows than you can imagine."

"That's no excuse," I said.

"No excuse. Just only remember, everybody's got something for a crutch, you know? It's a strange kind of life, creating art in a gin mill, working where everyone

149

else goes to play, where every night is Saturday night and Monday never comes. All right, he messed up more than most. But then he reached greater heights, too. And the one place where he was always honest was in his music."

Bronson was wearing a woven T-shirt. It looked orange, but it was really red and yellow chevrons. I kept looking at the chevrons.

"I'd like to hear you play sometime," he said. "I'd like to hear you play Linda Ann's music."

"I don't care anymore."

"I do. That's what I most truly care about. That's why Silk Garcia was worth nurturing."

"No," I said.

"He antagonized too many guys. At the end, he was down to playing clubs in SoHo, ten dollars a night off the books. He was living on food stamps. He had a monkey on his back. But even at the end, he was still stretching. He was experimenting with sitar and Indian music and . . ."

I couldn't listen to any more. I couldn't listen to any more about talent and genius and music.

"He tried to *sell* me!"

"He was living inside a nightmare then."

"I was his daughter!"

"You were the closest thing he had to some kind of connection."

"He knew where to find me."

"Having a child out there somewhere meant something to him."

"He never even tried to see me!"

"He couldn't."

"He never loved me! I was nothing to him!"

"Linda, he came up to my apartment a few weeks before he died. It was sometime in the middle of December." Bronson was standing with his arms dangling loosely at his sides. "I hadn't seen him for a while. His cheeks were hollow and his lips looked blue. It was cold out; it had been snowing and his coat was wet, but he didn't want to take it off. He was carrying a big box, a huge box, all wrapped up in shiny red paper and ribbons. He'd come up for a drink, and I gave him one.

" 'I have a daughter, you know,' he said.

" 'I know that, Silk,' I said. He was in terrible shape.

" 'Just a little thing, you know,' he said. His eyes were cloudy.

" 'You know what's in here, man? I bought her a doll,' he said, 'for Christmas.'

"And he went on to describe it. Opens and shuts eyes. Cries 'Mama.' Cost him sixty bucks at F.A.O. Schwarz. You could see he was feeling good describing it.

" 'Life-size,' he said. 'It's bigger than she is. She's just a little bit of a thing, you know.'

"I wasn't sure who he meant. I thought he might have another child someplace. I knew he'd been living with a woman up in Washington Heights.

"I said, 'Which daughter you talking about, Silk?'

" 'Linda Ann,' he said. 'That's the only one I got, man.'

" 'And how old is she now, Silk?'

" 'Don't know, she's just a little thing.'

" 'Silk,' I finally said, as gently as I could, 'she'd be pretty near grown up.'

"His eyes focused on me and he looked startled.

" 'Silk,' I said, 'she'd be in her teens now. You better not send her a doll.'

"He passed his hand slowly over his forehead. 'Yeah, man, right, I forgot.' He left the package behind, all bright and shiny with its Christmas wrapping. Later, Anita sent it to the collection for the kids in the hospital.

Maybe I should have let him send it to you, I don't know."

"No," I said. "You were right. It would have upset me." I bit my lip hard.

Bronson looked at me with sad, tired eyes.

"At the end," he said, "he was still trying to reach out somehow."

He turned to me at the door. "I'm sorry, Linda. No one ever wanted to hurt you." He went into the living room and gently closed the door behind him.

I could hear the sound of voices, his and Mom's. I thought of Bronson, his pained eyes, his massive body. At least fifty pounds overweight and living on candy mints. Everyone has some kind of crutch, he'd said. Well, I'd had a fairy-tale father, more perfect than any real father could have been, a legend to lean on.

I heard the clinking of the cups and plates. I could smell the coffee. It was making me hungry.

All I'd learned about Silk Garcia added up to fragments. I couldn't put together any kind of image. Great or evil, he was lost to me either way.

I swung my legs over the side of the bed. The floor was cool and smooth on my bare feet. I stood up, shaky, and I realized I hadn't been up for days. I took a bunch of deep breaths. There was no way I was going to cry.

I looked at the guitar across the room. From now on, I'd be making my own music.

Epilogue

I t was Ray Bronson who gave me this opportunity. The jazz congregation of St. Monica's is putting on an all-night benefit and there'll be top
musicians, performing and in the audience. Ray hesitated when he told me the catch: the only way he
could justify asking an unknown like to me play was
as Silk Garcia's daughter. There'll be people in the audience who loved Silk's music, and I'm expected to
play "Blues for Linda Ann." Ray said that something
good might come out of being heard by all those people, but he could understand if I refused. I did think
about it, for a long time. Now I'm standing in the
shadows, waiting to go on. There are musicians here
whose sounds are giving me shivers, and I'm happy to
be part of it.

I am in my senior year at North Bay High. I've been
playing lead guitar with a local group, Thin Ice, for
more than a year and we're getting most of the school
dances in the area. I still take classes at the Guitar Institute, and I've received a scholarship from the Manhattan
School of Music for next year. I'll be eighteen this June,
and I'll see if Dan Stein remembers me. So I'm hoping

to work and study in the city, and Mom and I will be moving to New York.

Mom. The good part of everything that happened is the change in Mom. She doesn't have to protect me from the truth about Silk Garcia anymore and we can talk to each other now. I guess it's time for her to be leaving North Bay; it's too full of old expectations. She's talking about finding some other kind of job in the city, something to do with fashion. She sounds hopeful, and I think she'll pick up her life again.

I hear from Jeff Breslow every once in a while. He left high school a year early and went to the University of Chicago, because Janet Craig was there. He was accepted as an accelerated, gifted student and if anyone from North Bay ever becomes famous, I think it will be Jeff. The university sounds like the right place for him and those who have something special.

I saw Michael Harrison during Easter vacation in the checkout line at the A&P. He said college was a blast and how was I and was I still playing the guitar. I said yes and he said that was good. He looked wonderful, tan and golden, and we smiled at each other between his six-packs and my cantaloupe and Wonder Bread. I admired the perfect arrangement of dazzling white teeth and knew it couldn't touch what I've found with Pat Calhoun.

Pat Calhoun. He has a crazy, offbeat sense of humor and his nose wrinkles when he laughs. He is honest to the point of being tactless and he is a vegetarian and he is into surfing and he is exciting to be with and . . . I'm still discovering all the things he is.

About Silk Garcia. Well, I don't think about him anymore. I'm me, not Silk Garcia's kid. There was a time when my dream of him gave me confidence when I needed it most. I guess the reality serves as a demonstration of everything I don't want to be. But I don't think about him anymore. That lost guy with the blue lips, carrying a bright red Christmas package, is a stranger, someone I can't even hate, someone I never knew. I'll get through tonight's gig and that'll be the end of it.

I am center stage now. I cannot see beyond the glaring circle of spotlight that is concentrated on me. Baby pink, I think, good color; I'm learning. I am sitting on a high stool, my left foot propped up on a rung, my guitar securely balanced on my knee. My hand is poised midair for a moment. I can hear the silence all around me. I can hear them waiting. I swore I would never play "Blues for Linda Ann" again, but that's what they expect tonight. That's what they want from me. So I go into the familiar opening measures. I cannot understand him. I cannot condone him. I cannot forgive him. But the pain in his music is real, whatever caused it, and I am feeling his pain now. This is for you, Silk Garcia. This is for you.

ERIKA TAMAR has written several books for young adults, including the recent novels *It Happened at Cecilia's* and *High Cheekbones*. Born in Vienna, Austria, she currently resides in New York City.